J. T. EDSON'S
FLOATING OUTFIT

The toughest bunch of Rebels that ever lost a war, they fought for the South, and then for Texas, as the legendary Floating Outfit of "Ole Devil" Hardin's O.D. Connected ranch.

MARK COUNTER was the best-dressed man in the West: always dressed fit-to-kill. **BELLE BOYD** was as deadly as she was beautiful, with a "Manhattan" model Colt tucked under her long skirts. **THE YSABEL KID** was Comanche fast and Texas tough. And the most famous of them all was **DUSTY FOG**, the ex-cavalryman known as the Rio Hondo Gun Wizard.

J. T. Edson has captured all the excitement and adventure of the raw frontier in this magnificent Western series. Turn the page for a complete list of Berkley Floating Outfit titles.

J.T. Edson

GUN WIZARD

Ⓑ®

BERKLEY BOOKS, NEW YORK

Originally printed in Great Britain by
Brown Watson Limited.

This Berkley book contains the complete
text of the original edition.
It has been completely reset in a typeface
designed for easy reading, and was printed
from new film.

GUN WIZARD

A Berkley Book / published by arrangement with
Transworld Publishers Ltd.

PRINTING HISTORY
Corgi edition published 1969
Berkley edition / September 1983
Second printing / August 1985

ISBN: 0-425-08033-1

A BERKLEY BOOK ® TM 757,375
Berkley Books are published by The Berkley Publishing Group,
200 Madison Avenue, New York, New York 10016.
The name "BERKLEY" and the stylized "B" with design
are trademarks belonging to Berkley Publishing Corporation.
PRINTED IN THE UNITED STATES OF AMERICA

CHAPTER ONE

Johnny Behan's Dilemma

Tombstone City, Arizona Territory. A hot, sprawling, wild and wide open town. The great mines, the Toughnut, the Contention and the others poured forth their wealth and sent their workers into town to spend wages. The cattle spreads of Cochise County, Texas John Slaughter, the Clantons, the McLauries paid off their hard-riding crews and most of that pay went over the many saloon bars in Tombstone City. From out Galeyville way, up in the hills, came the rustlers, happy-go-lucky followers of Curly Bill Brocious and Johnny Ringo. They came to Tombstone all these men, all with money in their pockets, money they wished to spend on fun, on gambling and occasionally on tweaking the nose of the local law.

Johnny Behan held post of sheriff for Cochise County; a stout, affable man who would have preferred politics to handling a law badge. He was a good lawman for all of that and willing to put up with a reasonable amount of hell-raising in the interests of greater peace and quiet.

Behan was a Democrat in a town which was mostly Re-

publican and had been put in office by the Territorial Governor
when Cochise County first was formed. This did not meet with
the approval of the Republican clan, so they formed the so
called Law and Order Party. Prominent amongst these public
spirited citizens were certain men who had gained something
of a name for themselves in the cattle towns of Kansas. They
were the Earp Brothers, Wyatt, Morgan, James and Virgil, the
latter being town marshal. They were a hard bunch and harder
with the backing of men like Bat Masterson, Sherman Mc-
Masters, Doc Holliday and their like.

The fast-growing town sat back and rubbed eager hands in
anticipation of what Johnny Behan would make of this devel-
opment. In this they were to be disappointed, for Behan was
far too loyal to his oath of office to involve in bickering and
trouble making with another officer of the law.

So things stood when the owners of the big mines produced
their inspiration, their idea to bring some fame—and not an
inconsiderable sum of Eastern money—to help further develop
their holdings.

They were rich men by any standards, these mine owners,
powerful men with an influence that reached to and beyond
the Territorial capital. In the way of rich and powerful men
they craved for the atmosphere of culture and refinement much
wealth demanded.

The Bon Ton Theatre at one time or another brought the
most talented and famous performers of the day to tread its
boards. The drama and noble words of Shakespeare, the thun-
dering notes of great operatic stars, the wail of some maestro's
violin at one time or another held entranced the mine owners
and their workers alike in this center of culture set in the heat
and dust of the Arizona hills.

The homes of the mine owners were as good as could be
found in any Eastern city. The meals they served were cooked
by chefs who had worked in the kitchens of great European
houses and their table service as good as could be found in the
land.

These then were the men who decided they would organise
and run the Cochise County Fair.

No ordinary county fair would do for them. For their glory

it must be the greatest, the most magnificent county fair ever held anywhere in the whole United States. There would be tests for cooking and preserve making for the womenfolk, a chance for them to display their talents with needle and dresscutting shears. For the men would be trials of speed in sinking a drill bit into the hard soil, contests with shovel and pick. There would be a prize-fight by two pugilists who were spoken of throughout the country. There would be contests for the cow-hands, too, riding bad-bucking horses, roping, throwing and hog-tying cattle. There would be a chuckwagon race which would attract great attention, for every ranch prided itself in the ability of its cook to handle the traces of a racing chuck-wagon team.

Not that the mine owners cared for such things, but they knew that to the Eastern visitor the cowhand had a glamour that the mine worker never had. There was another reason for the inclusion of the cowhand sports. John Slaughter, Texas John, ranched near Tombstone and would be quick to take offence at any slight to his loyal hands. Texas John was just as rich and autocratic as any mine owner and something of a power in the county. On no account must he be slighted in any way.

With their plans arranged, the mine owners were struck with a sudden thought. Nothing they were offering was different than could be shown at the fair of any county. Cochise County must offer something more, something which would be guar-anteed to bring the rich Easterners out West, where they might be persuaded to invest in the mines.

One of the owners came up with the suggestion of a rifle shoot. It would be a match that would attract the best shots in the West. Tests for skilled handling of repeating rifles more than for the long-ranged work of such weapons as the Sharps Old Reliable or the Remington Creedmore rifles. There was one prize which would bring in the best men and that would be the prize the Conchise County Fair would offer. So ac-cordingly an order was rushed to the Winchester Repeating Firearms Company for one of the specially constructed "One Thousand" Model of 1873 rifles.

An uneasy feeling came to the organizers of the Fair that

this match might be equalled and one of their number brought out the pièce-de-résistance, the idea which they were sure would make their fair a success.

In the East nothing was so talked about to do with the West than the speed and accuracy of the gunfighter with his Colt. The mine owners decided they would try and draw in the masters of the tied-down holster for a match. Put up such a prize as would draw the fast men to Tombstone to compete in a shooting match to prove who was the fastest and best shot of them all. The prize would be a pair of matched and gold inlaid Colt Peacemakers and a good sum of money also. There would be other prizes, for the Eastern firearms companies would donate freely so as to have their weapons on show before so large an audience. The shooting match would be as good a test of skill as could be arranged, long range shooting, handling guns with either or both hands, then if Colt's factory could fix it, a test to decide who was the fastest double draw of them all.

The news of the shooting match burst like a bomb over the West, spread by the telegraph wires and word of mouth and boosted in every newspaper throughout the wild range country. Within a month the names of fast men were coming in to be entered and if all held well the shooting match, the Fair along with it, would be a show long remembered in the West.

Johnny Behan saw in this apparently harmless Fair a threat to his office. There was soon to be an election for the post of County Sheriff and already Wyatt Earp was boasting he would claim the post. Earp stood high in the betting among the entrants for both rifle and pistol shooting and if he won would command a veritable landslide of votes. Earp, for all his faults, was a fine shot with rifle and fast with a revolver. Also he owned that long-barrelled Peacemaker presented to him by Ned Buntline and that would lend him a big advantage over the more conventional weapons used by his opponents.

Behan was no gunfighter, he could draw and shoot in about a second, but that was only rated as fast among people who'd never seen a real fast Western man in action. Such a man, and Earp was one, could almost halve that time and hit his man at the end of it. If Earp won the two, or even one, of the events he would be carried into office on the strength of it; then with his brother Virgil as town marshal, Tombstone would find itself under the heel of Kansas-trained lawmen.

There did not appear to be any way Behan could stop this happening. He knew he could never gain the lightning fast reactions and co-ordination of mind and muscle which went to make a real fast man with a gun. His deputies were brave and good men, but under no stretch of the imagination could they be termed fast. Burt Alvord was in town and highly fancied by some in both matches, but Behan could expect nothing from him. Alvord had been a Tombstone deputy until Behan fired him. The reason for the firing was that Alvord always brought his man in dead and was suspected of only bringing in such as could not pay their way by him. If the man could pay, there was more than a strong rumour that Alvord was not beyond escorting the man to the border and ensuring his safe crossing. If Behan enlisted the aid of such a man he would do himself more harm than good.

In desperation Behan put the problem to Texas John Slaughter, but received no sympathy or offer of aid. Slaughter believed in staying out of his neighbour's feuds and making sure he was respected for it. So the rancher had no intention of becoming involved in the political and office seeking feuds of the town— then he overheard Wyatt Earp boasting he would win both shooting matches, become sheriff and that those trouble-causing cowhands best watch out.

Slaughter made no reply, although he knew the challenge was directed at his head. He was not afraid; that small, tough rancher did not know where fear was kept, but he knew blood would be shed if he took Earp up on it. Instead of picking up the gauntlet, John Slaughter held his peace and headed for the telegraph office. What message he sent and to whom was never mentioned by the old timer who worked the key, even though the said old timer found the occasional ten dollar gold piece under his message pad on the unsaid understanding he not let the Earp brothers know anything to their advantage or disadvantage. John Slaughter said nothing about the message either— but then he never did.

It was a fortnight to the day before the County Fair opened. Tombstone was already booming wide open at the seams and every stagecoach brought in more people. The rooming houses and hotels were either full or booked to capacity, every house filled with paying guests.

The Bucket of Blood Saloon was among the best in town, standing proudly on Contention Street. However, at this early hour of the morning it was empty of all but a lone bartender idly polishing glasses. He stood behind the long, shiny and polished bar which was his pride and joy, surveying the tables, the covered-over vingt-et-un, roulette and tiger-decorated faro layouts. His eyes went to the free lunch counter which was already set out for the customers. He turned and glanced at the display of bottles on the shelves which surrounded the mirror. A man could buy anything from root-beer to fine champagne in the Bucket of Blood. Turning, the bartender glanced at the stage to one side, with the pit for the three-piece orchestra before it. He nodded with approval, all in all Buckskin Frank Leslie's Bucket of Blood saloon stood up to a standard which would not have disgraced New York or Chicago.

The bartender was sure of that, he'd been imported from the East to take charge of the bar, instead of the leathery, stove-up old cowhand who usually fulfilled this honoured post. He was a man well skilled in his trade and had served drinks in good quality bars in New York and Chicago's Streeterville section. He could mix any of the better known drink combinations, serve them with style. He could chat amiably yet respectfully with the richest and touchiest customer, handle a rowdy drunk with either tact or muscle, depending on the drunk's financial standing; he could slip undetected a mickey finn into the drink of a dangerous customer—but he did not know cowhands.

The batwing doors opened and three men entered, three young Texas cowhands. The bartender's eyes went to them and saw nothing but the bare essentials. The low-crowned, wide-brimmed, J. B. Stetson hats, the clothes, the high-heeled, expensive, made-to-measure boots, the way they wore their guns, all told a story to a man who knew the West. To the bartender they were just three cowhands fresh in from the range.

Two of the men would have caught the eye in any company for all that. One of them, mused the bartender, would be about as fine a looking man as he'd ever seen. Full three inches more than six foot this man, even without the aid of his Kelly spurred boots or the costly white Stetson with the silver concha decorated band. He towered over his friends, his golden-blond hair combed neatly, his face almost classically handsome. His shoulders were broad in a great muscular spread which strained the tailored tan shirt, as did the powerful biceps of his arms. His cowhand style brown levis hung outside his boots with the cuffs turned back, his legs were long, straight, powerful and stood over the ground as if they owned it. Around his waist, hanging just right, was a brown leather gunbelt and in the holsters which were tied to his legs, ivory grips flaring so that his hands could reach them, were a brace of Colt Cavalry model Peacemakers. Fine looking guns, but plain, well cared-for fighting man's weapons.

The second of the eye-catching pair was not quite as tall, or as broad as the handsome blond giant. He was lean, lithe and gave the impression of having whipcord strength. All in black was this boy dressed, from hat to boots. Even the leather of his gunbelt was black and the only relief to the blackness came in the ivory hilt of the bowie knife at his left side and the worn walnut grips of the old Colt Second Model Dragoon revolver which was butt forward at his right. His hair was so black it almost shone blue in the light as he thrust back his Stetson. His face was young looking, innocent appearing and almost babyishly handsome. It was the face of a delicately reared youth in his teens—until a man looked at the eyes. They were cold eyes, old eyes, red hazel in colour. They were not the eyes to go with such a face.

The third man of the trio was smaller and the bartender hardly gave him a second glance. He was small, insignificant in appearance, not more than five foot six in height. His hair was a dusty colour, his hat thrust back from it. His face was tanned, handsome though not eye-catching. His grey eyes looked straight at a man without flinching. His mouth looked as if it would smile easily yet without any weakness and the face itself showed some strength. His figure was powerful, despite his lack of inches, his clothes were good quality, but he did not set them off as did his taller friends. His hat and boots had cost good money, as had that buscadero gunbelt with the matched white-handled Colt Civilian Peacemakers which were butt forward in the holsters.

Crossing the room, the three men halted at the bar before the bartender. "We'll take a beer each, friend," drawled the blond giant. "And call up a drink for yourself."

The bartender noticed the voice and accent. It was a deep, cultured Southern drawl, not the tone of a working cowhand.

"Would you gents be in for the County Fair?" asked the bartender as he served out the drinks with deft hands.

"We surely are, Colonel," answered the dark youngster.

The bartender was impressed by the pleasing tenor quality of the voice, but those eyes were disconcerting. There was something wild, alien, Indian almost, about them, which went with the free-striding way the young man crossed the room. It was almost as if he glided and gave the impression he could pass over heat-dried sticks without making a sound.

"Where'd a man enter for the events, happen he wanted to?" inquired the small man, glancing at the two big blackboards behind the bar. Each blackboard carried a list of names with the betting odds opposite each one.

"Right here's as good a place as any, although you can enter in any of the saloons. What'll it be for you, roping?"

"Not for us," replied the dark boy with a grin. "I never took to ropes since Uncle Obidiah died dancing."

"What'd ropes have to do with that?" demanded the bartender, playing his part by falling for the coming joke.

"He was dancing at the end of one."

The bartender joined in the laugh, then went on, "How about hoss busting?"

"That's all right for a man with a strong back, hard bones and a weak head," answered the big blond. "Which same I've only got the weak head."

"Well, I'll hazard a guess you're not interested in drill driving, hammer swinging or digging. I don't reckon pie making or dress sewing's much in your line either. Don't leave much else except the eating contest—or the shooting."

The three cowhands looked gravely at the bartender and he looked just as gravely back. Then they gave their attention to the two blackboards and studied the names of the contestants. The top men in both rifle and pistol shooting fields were already showing on the lists.

"Mr. Earp looks tolerable well favoured," said the dark boy

sardonically. "Stands at even money for both. Look at that list.
Tom Horn, Burt Alvord, old Steve Venard. Now there's three
dandy cards to sit in with on the deal. It's like to scare a poor
lil Texas boy out'n trying. Still, I've come this far so I might
as well go in and make a fool of myself. Set me down on the
board there, friend."

"What name'd it be, friend?" queried the bartender.

"Loncey Dalton Ysabel. What odds are you calling for lil
ole me?"

That put the bartender in something of a quandary. His boss
usually attended to the adjustment of odds, for Leslie knew by
name or reputation every man who entered and could gauge
his chances. At this moment Leslie was out meeting the troupe
of show folks he'd brought in as a special drawing card for the
County Fair.

"Let's say three to one, shall we?" he finally asked, making
his choice with care. The odds were not high enough to arouse
interest yet short enough to show the dark youngster no slight
to his talents was meant. If they were wrong, Leslie could soon
alter them on his return.

"Allow me to get some of that, friend," said the big blond
and laid a ten dollar gold piece on the table. "Are you taking
the bets?"

"That's my pleasure," grinned the bartender, accepting the
money and making out the receipt for it. "What're you aiming
to go in for?"

"Pistol shooting."

"What's the name, friend. I'll start you in at the same three
to one."

"Mark Counter, and what odds on my standing second or
third?"

"Leave it at the same three to one," answered the bartender,
pleased to be making his boss some money. He marked the
names on the board, then turned to the small man. "What'll
you be trying for, mister?"

"Reckon I'll have a whirl for those fancy old gold mounted
Colt guns too."

The smile died for a moment, then returned to the bartender's face. He understood. The small cowhand was wanting to
make everyone notice him by entering for the Pistol Shoot.

"All right," boomed the bartender, wishing there was more of a crowd to share in the joke. "If that's what you want, that's what you get. Service with a smile, that's the motto of the Bucket of Blood. I reckon we'd best start you in at ten to one. We can always bring it down later."

In that the bartender hoped the small cowhand would take the hint that he was way out of his depth in entering the match. The three Texans exchanged glances, then two pairs of startled eyes turned to the bartender.

"Ten to one?" croaked Mark Counter.

"You mean ten to one he *don't* win?" went on Loncey Dalton Ysabel in a strangled croak of amazement.

"Sure, you didn't reckon I meant one to ten, did you?"

For a moment the two men stared at each other, then as if fearing the bartender would change his mind they dipped their hands into their pockets. Fifty dollars each of them placed on the counter and demanded the sum be scooped up and accepted. The bartender thought the two cowhands were going to costly lengths for a laugh. He started to write out the receipts on slips when a thought came to him.

Looking up at the small Texan, he grinned and said, "You know, I never got your name, friend."

The small man studied the bartender, a smile flickered on his face, while his two friends stood by with mocking eyes, waiting for the shock which was coming.

"I didn't tell you—but it's Dusty Fog."

CHAPTER TWO

On the Tombstone Trail

"Hello the camp. Can we ride through the water?"

Dusty Fog brought his big paint stallion to a halt as he called out the time-honoured range request for permission to approach a camp. Mark Counter, lounging in the double-girthed Texas rig of his seventeen hand bloodbay stallion, restrained the eagerness of the packhorse he led to get to the ford. The Ysabel Kid sat his huge stallion at Dusty's other side, graceful and relaxed afork a horse which was large and mean enough looking to scare a man.

It was the etiquette of the range that one called a greeting before riding into camp. The two covered wagons on the other side was a camp. There was a fire going, the scent of coffee and stew wafting on the breeze towards the three Texans. Around the fire stood three men and half a dozen women and it was one of them who turned to call out a reply:

"Come ahead and rest your saddles."

Dusty studied the people as he started his paint stallion

across the stream. The party, in their camp up the slope, were not what he'd expect to see out on the open range country. A family of sod-busting nesters looking for a piece of new land might be out here. A bunch of miners traveling from Tombstone in search of work, a ranch trail crew returning from a drive, any of these might be out on the range. These folk were none of those categories.

The men wore stylishly cut Eastern clothes, it showed even though they were in shirt sleeves, or two of them were. The women, with one exception, were dressed in rather colourful and modish frocks which were not the wear of poor nester wives. These were show people unless Dusty missed his guess. Not a medicine show either, the wagons were too plain for that. These would be real showfolks, carrying their own scenery and props in the wagons with them. He was sure he could remember the big, henna haired, statuesque woman who called the reply to him, but he could not yet place her.

Swinging down from his horse, Mark Counter removed his white hat and bowed gracefully to honour the ladies, even though some of the party might not be such ladies at all.

"Howdy, folks," he greeted.

"Good afternoon, young men," answered the big woman coolly, studying them all with some care.

"Take it kind if we could night here with you, ma'am," Dusty said as he came from his saddle. "This's the best camp spot along the river. We've food in our pack saddle."

"Join us by all means," replied the woman. Her voice and actions were those of someone who was used to being seen and admired. "And don't worry about food. Cindy there always cooks theatre style, with plenty and to spare for all."

The girl by the fire looked around from the pot she was attending to. She was different from the other four girls who lounged about the camp. They were no different to the hostesses of any decent saloon or dance hall of any big Western town. She was tall, willowy, yet with a rich, entirely feminine figure which her modest gingham dress could not hide. Her hair was blonde, taken back shoulder long in a style which was attractive and yet not fussy. Her face was sweet, gentle and very pretty, with only the very lightest touch of make-up. Her smile of welcome was different from the interested glances the other girls directed towards Dusty, Mark and the Kid.

The three Texans attended to their mounts, stripping off the heavy double girthed Texas rigs and allowed the horses to go free and graze. Mark attended to the pack horse before they came back towards the fire.

The big woman was watching them with some interest still, a puzzled frown on her face. Then she smiled and came forward, extending a hand on which good rings glittered.

"I never forget a face," she said. "You're Captain Dusty Fog, aren't you?"

"That's right enough, Ma'am," Dusty agreed. "You'll likely remember Mark and the Kid here, they were in Mulrooney with me while you were there."

Now the four flashily dressed girls showed more interest. Those three names were well enough known throughout the West.

Dusty Fog, that small, insignificant and soft talking young man. Here stood a man who did not look the part his reputation called for. In the War Between the States, at seventeen, Dusty had carved himself a name which ranked with Turner Ashby and John Singleton Mosby as a fast riding light cavalry leader. Since the war Dusty's name came to rank with the tophands of the cattle business. He was the segundo of the OD Connected, Ole Devil Hardin's great Rio Hondo ranch and leader of Ole Devil's floating outfit, the handiest and toughest men of a handy and tough crew. Men spoke of Dusty Fog as trail boss, as town taming lawman and as being the peer of any of the wizards of the tied-down holster. They told how he brought law to Quiet Town, to Mulrooney, the wild trail end city. Whatever they told, it was all true. That was Dusty Fog, a giant among men despite his lack of inches.

Mark Counter had also carved himself something of a name throughout the cattle country. He was a tophand the equal of, if not better, than Dusty Fog. He was known as a fist fighter who could handle any man on any terms. They told of his giant strength, but they never mentioned his skill with his guns. A few, a very select few claimed he was almost as fast as Dusty Fog with his matched long-barrelled Colt guns. Beyond this select handful there were few enough whom could say how good Mark was with his guns, for he lived in the shadow of the Rio Hondo gun-wizard, Dusty Fog.

The Ysabel Kid, the last of the trio. Now there was a name to conjure with down on the Rio Grande. They once spoke of him as a one boy crime-wave, a border smuggler who knew every trail along the big river. He was the son of a wild Irish-Kentuckian father and a French-Creole-Comanche mother, and from that admixture of wild bloods came forth a dangerous young hell-twister. From his father's side he gained a love of fighting and the sighting eye of a woodsman of old. From his mother he inherited the ability to ride any horse that ever walked, to follow a track and ride scout among the best. From her French-Creole side also came a love for cold steel as a fighting weapon and the ability to handle his bowie kife in a manner of the man who designed it. All-in-all the Ysabel Kid was a fighting man with a skill beyond his years and far beyond his innocent appearance.

"I remember you," replied the big woman. "I'm Paula Raymond. Come and meet the rest of my people."

The introductions followed quickly. Paula Raymond was an actress and a good one, but she was never one to allow anybody to take her place in the center of things. The big, burly man with the heavy moustaches so necessary to a stage villain was her husband, Joe. The old man in the frock coat was a Shakespearean actor down on his luck and reduced to playing in low drama. He was distant as became one who had appeared on New York stages. The four gaily dressed girls were just called by their first names as being of insufficient importance to receive full introductions. That left the tall, wide-shouldered, tanned and handsome young man and the blonde girl to be presented.

"This is Miles Hamish, our hero," Paula said.

Hamish held out his hand, his grip was firm. Actor he might be, but there were hard muscles in his arms. He was clearly on his dignity, not willing to accept the cowhands as friends or anything but admirers.

"And of course the star, the female star," Paula went on, making the correction as there was just the smallest tightening of Hamish's lips at the words, "Cindy Alban."

The girl came from the fire with a warm smile on her face as she held out a hand to Dusty first, then each of the others.

The three cowhands were polite, restrained in their greetings.
To the other four girls they would have extended the same free
and easy kind of friendship they'd given to the saloon girls of
many a town. Cindy Alban was different. She was a girl a man
dreamed about as he rode the circle around a trail herd in the
Indian Nations when the stars shone down and the cattle lay
bedded for the night.

"I'm pleased to meet you, gentlemen," she said in a voice
which was gentle and pleasant.

"You're sure we're not putting you to any inconvenience,
ma'am?" Dusty asked. "We've got food here in the pack and
it won't take us but a minute to throw some in the pot."

"We wouldn't hear of it, Captain Fog," Paula answered.
Clearly it was she who ran the troupe and made all the decisions.
"We've enough for you."

"More than enough," Cindy agreed. "If you gentlemen would
like to freshen up before the meal, I'm sure Miles will show
you the place he used in the bushes there."

"Leave your saddles and wagons, boys," Joe Raymond put
in. "You can either bunk down under the wagons with us men,
or you can sleep by the fire."

"We'll use the fire, I reckon," Dusty answered. "It'd be a
mite cramped under the wagon and ole Mark here snores like
to wake the dead."

"Have it your way, then," Raymond replied and turned to
discuss some point of stage procedure with the old man.

"You're a mite away from Kansas, ma'am," Mark drawled
after they'd put the saddles by the wagons and dug out their
washing and shaving gear.

"That we are. We've just played a most successful season
in Texas and received a call from our friend Buckskin Frank
Leslie to be his stars for the Cochise Country Fair. He also
offers us a fortnight at the Bon Ton Theatre before the Fair,
so we came along."

"Have you ever been to Tombstone?" asked one of the girls.

"Not for a year. We ran a herd of cattle out here for Texas
John last year, just after the town started to boom wide-open
at the seams," Mark replied.

"What's it like?"

"Wild, woolly, full of fleas and never curried below the

knees, gal," drawled the Kid. "Just like Quiet Town, up in Montana after the War. Or Dodge, Mulrooney, Wichita or any of the trail end towns when the herds came in. Only with Tombstone the seasons lasts seven days a week, every week of the year."

"It'll be worse than ever with the County Fair coming off," Dusty went on. "I reckon every card-sharp, cheap hold-up man and would-be fast gun in the West will be headed there for the pickings."

Paula looked at the three young men. She'd seen the wild towns and from what Dusty Fog just said she knew she could expect some trouble in Tombstone. The other towns had been wild when the trail drive crews paid off, but the wilderness drew off between drives. In Tombstone it never died down and with the County Fair the pace would be increased.

"Are you entering for any of the County Fair events?" she inquired.

"I don't know, ma'am," Dusty replied. "I reckon we might be. Texas John asked Uncle Devil to send us along to win some of the prizes if we can."

"We were unsure of the advisability of calling off our Texas bookings," Paula remarked thoughtfully. "Even though Frank's terms are most liberal. However, he is an old friend, so we came along. The towns we have passed through on the way here don't give me any great hopes for Tombstone."

"Don't let them fool you, ma'am," warned the Kid. "Why, Tombstone's as fancy as Dodge City or Chicago."

Cindy looked up from the fire. "If you gentlemen wish to wash up before eating, you'd best go now. Are you going, Miles?"

"I just came back," Hamish answered.

"Reckon we can find the water, ma'am," drawled the Kid.

The three young men walked from the camp, down the slope and were soon in the bushes which lined the small stream. They had made a dry camp the previous night and so were in need of a wash and shave. The stream water was cold, but all three of them were used to washing and shaving in cold water. Mark stropped his razor, stripped to the waist, his mighty torso writhing with muscles. Watching them, the Kid grinned. The Kid scorned such affectations as shaving soap, lather brush and

azor. To shave his needs were simple, water, the soap he used
or washing and the edge of his bowie knife.

The horses had grazed down the slope towards the bushes
nd the big white was more like a wild animal than a domes-
icated beast. It never relaxed and repeatedly tested the wind
vith its nostrils as it grazed.

"Supaway, John?"

Paula Raymond looked up as the words were called from
he slope above the camp. She heard startled gasps as the rest
»f the troupe saw who their callers were. Six ragged looking
oung Apaches sat their horses and looked down at the camp.
The greeting they'd called was the usual one an Indian would
;ive when approaching a camp in search of a meal.

"What tribe are you?" demanded Raymond.

This was a sensible precaution to take, or would have been
vith the semi-tamed Indians of the Oklahoma Territory. They
vere the kind of Indians Raymond was used to, the tribes which
vere under the firm heel of the reservation agents and the
:avalry.

"We Lipan Apache," growled the squat, scar-faced buck
who sat his horse ahead of the others. "Not bad Indians, we
riends to all white-eyes."

Raymond knew that the Lipans were a branch of the Apache
Nation, one which lived to the east of the main fighting tribes
nd one which had never taken up the war bow against the
white man. They should be safe enough to allow into the camp.
Iis eyes went to the men, noting that they were all young and
he only weapons they appeared to have were the hunting knives
n their belts.

"Come ahead," he finally said.

With the reservation Indians of the Oklahoma Territory it
was always as well to invite them in for a meal. It saved trouble,
or the braves could turn nasty if they were crossed, especially
when away from the eye of authority. However, with the reservation Indians a few trinkets, some tobacco and food were
:nough to satisfy them and get rid of them. That was where
Raymond made his mistake. He was no longer in Oklahoma
Territory, he was in Arizona, almost the last frontier of the bad
white-hating Indian.

The braves rode nearer, then dropped from their horses in

the relaxed and easy way of their kind. They advanced on th
fire, fanning out in a casual and innocent appearing manner
their faces blank of expression but their eyes on the white
people.

"You want food?" Paula asked.

"We want plenty food," replied the squat brave. "No make
trouble for white-eyes if they give us plenty food, tobacco—
and guns."

That gave a warning to Raymond. There was something
bad wrong here. The braves were altogether too at ease and
truculent. He did not like the way they came on towards the
fire.

"We'll give you plenty food," he answered. "Tobacco. But
we don't have any guns."

"No guns, huh?"

"No guns," Raymond agreed, spreading his arms and show
ing his gunless sides.

"That good," growled the scar-faced brave, then snapped
an order in his own language.

At the words every Apache whipped out his knife and leap
towards the white people around the fire. There was sudden
confusion, the three men jumping forward to try and protec
the women, the four chorus girls running for the wagons, while
Paula swung a wild hand which knocked the nearest brave to
her staggering. Cindy Alban was nearest to the Apaches. She
saw the scar-faced brave lunge forward and twisted to one side
His clawing hand touched the shoulder of her dress in passing
then she was free and running and he was after her. The girl
saw him, looking back over her shoulder, saw she was cut off
from the wagons and fled down the slope into the bushes.

Around the fire there was wild confusion. Raymond flung
himself forward, his fist landing hard on the face of a brave
Hamish saw Cindy's peril but he was forced back by the attack
of a knife-slashing brave. With remarkable agility the old actor
avoided the rush of a wild young brave, tripped him and was
tackled by another. It was a wild mêlé, but there would have
been only one end to it had there not been help and very efficient
help on hand.

By the stream Dusty, Mark and the Kid had finished their
ablutions and were collecting their gear together. They were

relaxed, discussing the chance meeting, when from the open the Kid's white stallion suddenly threw back its shapely head and gave an angry snort.

"Apaches!"

The one word came from the Kid in a Comanche-deep grunt. He took in the half-dozen braves with Indian-wise eyes, noting particularly the youth of the party, their lack of weapons and reading the signs right. This was a bunch of marauding young bucks on their first war trail, out after loot. They would not risk much in the way of a fight, at least until they were better armed. Raymond and his party would be safe enough as long as they kept up a bold front, gave some small tribute and did not let——

"Hell fire!" growled the Kid. "He's letting them into the camp. Get back there and *pronto!*"

That was the one thing Raymond should have resisted at all cost, allowing the bucks to get into the camp and see how poorly armed the troupe were. Feed them, give them tobacco, but never should Raymond have allowed them to get in close.

The attack started as the three Texans sprinted up the slope. Cowhand boots were never meant for running in, but for all of that the three were making good time. Then the Kid saw Cindy fleeing along the slope above him, saw her and the following brave disappear into the bushes and swung off at a tangent. Dusty and Mark could handle the other braves. The Kid was going to be needed far more by that pretty girl with the gentle smile.

Raymond leapt backwards, avoiding the slashes of the brave who was after him. He was no fool and had been in more than one brawl, but this time Raymond was up against a man who meant to kill him. He watched his chance, ready to slam home his hard fists, but did not get a chance. Hamish had the wrist of a second brave gripped and they were rolling over and over on the floor, each trying to get the other in a position where he could be finished. The old man went down under a third brave, the knife rose and drove down at the front of his old frock coat. Then the brave gave a startled yell, for his knife point sank in about half an inch and came to a stop. The old actor gave a sudden heave which threw the Apache from him and he rolled over, the bound copy of the Works of Shakespeare falling from his jacket. It had done its work by taking the force of the blow and preventing the knife from sinking home.

The women were backed against the wagons and two of the braves came at them, knives in hand ready for use. Paula clenched her hands but the four girls behind her, screaming in terror and clinging to her, prevented her from doing anything.

It was at that moment Dusty Fog and Mark Counter came on to the scene. They came through the bushes at just the right moment. Young Hamish's head hit the ground hard, he was dazed and the Apache tore free his knife hand, rearing up as he drew back the knife.

Dusty's left-hand Colt came out and roared in one flickering movement. Fast though the move was the Apache kneeling astride Hamish was caught by the bullet, jerked backwards and went down. Even before the Apache's body had hit the ground a second one, Raymond's attacker, crumpled and went down before the long-barrelled Cavalry Peacemaker in Mark Counter's right hand.

The two braves who were after the girls and the third, crouching to attack the old actor, saw the two men from the bushes, saw them and knew that no longer was this a safe game to play. They broke off the attack, sprinting for their horses and leaping astride the bare backs with an agility that was a joy to watch. One of them whipped back his hand, his knife raised to throw. Dusty and Mark both fired at the same moment and the young Indian was knocked flying from his horse, dead before his body struck the ground. Either bullet would have killed him.

Then the attack was over and the two living braves raced for safety. Raymond threw a glance to see if his wife was safe and turned a pale face towards Hamish and the old actor. Hamish was on his hands and knees, shaking his head to clear it and the old man was clucking his tongue as he studied the battered old book.

With the people of the troupe unhurt Raymond turned to look at his rescuers. He opened his mouth to say something as Paula pushed free of the hysterical girls and came towards the men. The words were never said. From the bushes came the sound of a shrill scream, then the most blood-curdling yell any of them had ever heard.

"What was that?" gasped Raymond, his face even paler.

Mark Counter pumped the empty cartridge case from the ejection gate of his Colt and slipped a fresh bullet in to replace it. "That was a dead mean ole Comanche getting riled up."

"Comanche!" yelped the showman. "They said they were Apaches."

"They were," agreed Mark.

It was at that moment all of them realized that Cindy was not in the camp.

"Cindy!" Paula screamed. "It's Cindy. He's got her. Get after her!"

Dusty and Mark did not move, they remained where they were loading their guns. "One way or another, ma'am," Dusty answered. "It's too late for that now."

Cindy had fled from the camp, running as she'd never run before. Behind her she could hear the patter of the Apache's moccasined feet as he chased her. The squat buck was not agile and the girl managed to keep away from his reaching, clawing hands, although she and he knew it was only a matter of time. They were in the bushes now, and the girl felt a branch strike her, then her foot caught in a root and she went down, rolling under a small bush. With terrified eyes she looked up at the leering, savage face of the Apache close on her. A scream broke from her throat, rose high and then ended abruptly.

There was a rush of feet and a black shape arrived in the open behind the Apache. Cindy's ears were jarred by a hideous yell which rang out from the black dressed apparition. It was a man Cindy dully thought she should recognize, a man whose black clothing was familiar but whose face was such as she'd never seen before. It was the hard fighting mask of a Comanche Dog Soldier and the yell was the coup cry of that same wild fighting warrior from the Texas plains.

The Apache also saw this sight of an Indian's face in white man's clothing. Saw it and the eleven and a half inch bowie knife blade which ripped at him. He started to make his parry, doing it with a speed which would have handled the attack of a white man—but it was not a white man who struck at him. It was the grandson of Chief Long Walker of the Comanches, war leader of the dread Dog Soldier Lodge who launched the knife blow, and the Apache never saw the day when he could teach a Comanche anything to do with the noble art of fighting with a knife.

Just a vital split-second too late the Apache began his parry and from then on it was all over. The great blade, sharper than many a barber's razor, went under the Apache's guard and sank home, biting into the knife-fighter's favourite target, the belly. The Kid felt his knife go home and ripped it across, feeling the hot rushing gush of blood against his hand, saw the Apache's face take on an expression of agony and drew back his hand. The knife blade was red in the Kid's hand and the Apache folded over, clutching at the middle as he went to the ground.

For a moment the Kid stood, allowing the wild Comanche blood to settle again. He tried to fight down the reckless streak of Indian in him but never, when he held a knife and faced an enemy, could he. Bending forward, he wiped the knife blade clean on the Apache's breechcloth, then straightened and looked at the girl who was crawling weakly from under the bush.

"You all right, Miss Cindy?" he asked. "I surely hope I didn't scare you too much."

The girl twisted towards him, recognizing him through the tears and the hysteria which welled up inside her. Desperately she tried to keep her eyes from the twitching, blood-oozing thing on the ground. She looked at the innocent, babyishly handsome face as if she could not believe her eyes. The clothes were the same but it appeared that an entirely different man had rescued her.

Then the reaction set in and with a cry Cindy flung herself into the Kid's arms and sobbed against his black shirt. He held her for a moment until she was over the worst of it and then turned her towards the camp.

"They told us they were Lipans," Raymond explained to the angry Kid who had brought Cindy back and turned her over to Paula, then demanded why the men had been fool stupid enough to let the Apaches get that close to them.

"Lipans?" barked the Kid. "Mister, they were Mogollons and real bad hats too."

"It's lucky we happened along," Dusty went on. "Let's get those bodies away from the camp and then we can eat."

It would not have mattered if Cindy had not cooked enough food to go around for only the three Texans felt like eating anything. The rest of them retired to the wagons and did not appear until night and even then they did not show any great desire to eat.

CHAPTER THREE

Mr. Earp Renews An Acquaintance

Buckskin Frank Lesile stepped from the side walk and advanced to meet the two wagons and the three Texas men who approached him. The time was ten o'clock and the saloon keeper was going to meet his friends Paula and Joe Raymond. He'd had one of his swampers out on trail for the past two days looking for the wagons and on hearing of their approach came forth to greet his friends.

People going about their business stopped to look at the wagons and their escort with interest. Madame Paula knew the value of publicity and had the canopy off the lead wagon and all her troupe dressed in their show costumes in the back, with the exception of her husband, who drove the second wagon. Hamish, dressed in a fancy buckskin outfit drove the first one; he saw that the eyes of Tombstone's young ladies were on him and for once the feeling worried him. He had not said much since the fight with the Apaches and felt that he could have shown better in it. The four chorus girls and, to a lesser degree, Cindy, had shown much interest in the three Texas men who saved them and Hamish felt a little jealous. Always on the stage he played the handsome hero, saving Cindy from a foul plot of the villain. Then for the first time when he could have played the hero in real life he failed. Seeing Cindy laughing and joking with her rescuer he felt for the first time an awareness of her. No longer was she just a first-class competent actress who played her scenes without tantrums or trying to steal everything on the stage. Now she was a very real women and Hamish wished he had shown better when his chance came.

Buckskin Frank raised his hand in greeting. He was a tall, slender man dressed to the height of frontier gambler's fashion except that he wore a fringed buckskin jacket instead of the more normal cutaway coat. For all that the gunbelt around his waist was no ornament and the white handled Colt Artillery Peacemaker was a tool of speed and precision in his hands.

"Welcome to Tombstone, Madame Paula," he boomed out in a voice which attracted the crowd and started them to gather. His eyes flickered to the three Texans, a glimmer of recognition in them. Then he got down to business. His old friends Dusty Fog, Mark Counter and the Ysabel Kid would not mind his ignoring them for the moment and there would be time to talk of the old days later. Turning to the fast gathering crowd he announced, "Ladies and gentlemen of Tombstone. As always I am bringing you the best entertainment possible. From tonight, until the start of the County Fair, Madame Paula's Talented Troupe will be presenting the latest drama plays at the Bon Ton Theatre and appearing in the Bucket of Blood Saloon. Now, presenting to you, Madame Paula Raymond——"

Dusty, Mark and the Kid backed off their horses to allow the show people the limelight. Leslie introduced the members of the troupe, doing it with a flair and shine that showed he was no mean showman himself. He saw the crowd growing and so saved Cindy until last. The girl would be a prime drawing card and would bring in the sentimental cowhand and mine worker's trade. She would be the sort of girl they dreamed about and would pay good money to see rescued from the clutches of the vile villain of the play.

Gallantly Leslie handed each of the girls down and shook hands with the men. Then he held out his hand, introduced Cindy and assisted her from the wagon box. The girl had barely set feet in the dusty road of Tombstone when a voice spoke from the front of the crowd.

"Introduce me to the lady, Leslie."

Leslie turned on his heel to look the speaker over, although he did not need to do so. The man stepping forward was well enough known to Leslie. He was a tall, slim and handsome young man, his face tanned, although he did not have the look or the dress of an outdoor man. He wore an expensive black cutaway coat, frilly white shirt, string tie, fancy vest, white trousers and shoes. His hat was a good Stetson but he did not have the flair of a Western man in how he wore it. He also wore a fast man's gunbelt but to eyes which could call the signs he was not fast with it.

Behind this elegant dandy stood two men of a type Leslie and the three Texans knew well. They wore cowhand clothes, belted guns and these were what they worked with. They were hired guns, the sort a man would take on when he could not get good stock.

Slowly Leslie released the girl's hand and stepped away from her. The onlookers in the crowd started to fade back leaving the handsome man and his two hired guns clear to view. Every member of the crowd was suddenly prepared to hunt for cover—fast.

"I said introduce me," the handsome young man went on.

"I'd as soon introduce her to a Digger Indian."

There was a sudden reddening of the handsome man's face. His hand lifted, his fingers spread as they hovered above the butt of the gun. Leslie watched the man, saw the two gunmen moving slowly to be clear of their boss and sensed that Dusty, Mark and the Kid were moving their horses to a place where they could back him if backing was needed.

"Introduce me, Leslie," said the man.

"You go to hell, Rambeau."

The show people were seeing something they'd seen before and knew what they must do. Paula was first off the mark, gently gripping Cindy's arm and moving her back out of the possible line of fire. At the same moment the woman blocked Hamish who had started to move forward. The young actor saw his chance to make up for his failure on the trail. He meant to step in and demand the man called Rambeau to take himself off hurriedly. The young actor could fight but only with his fists in a rough-house brawl. He would have as little chance here if guns began to roar as a snowball had of keeping shape on a hot stove top.

Slowly King Rambeau's eyes went to the three Texans as they slouched comfortably in their saddles in a half circle behind Leslie. His lips drew back in a sneering grin which made the handsome face look evil as the devil himself.

"Took to hiring guns now, Leslie?" he asked.

"What're those two behind you, *hombre?*" asked the Ysabel Kid mildly. "A couple of Tombstone churchwardens?"

Rambeau's eyes lifted to the Kid, seeing there was no mildness in his face no matter how his voice sounded. "Tough boy, huh? Take that worn old relic of a gun from him, boys."

"Start right in any time you like, gents," offered the Kid. He was not a fast man with a gun but he knew he was able to deal with either of the hired men and their boss.

The gunmen made no move. They knew the signs and they read the warning in that gentle, mocking face. It was as menacing as the purr of a cougar with a belly full of horsemeat.

It was then the crowd parted and a tall, solemn-looking man came forward. In dress he looked like a prosperous trail end town undertaker and his moustached face was familiar. Round his waist was a gunbelt with a black handled Colt Civilian Peacemaker at his right side. At his left was the twelve-inch barrelled special Colt presented to him by Ned Buntline. The crowd stirred with expectation for King Rambeau was a crony of Wyatt Earp—and Frank Leslie was not.

Behind Earp, on the sidewalk, stood his brother Virgil, looking much the same and with the shield of town marshal on his jacket lapel for all to see. His face showed nothing of whether he approved or disapproved of what Brother Wyatt was doing.

Equally inscrutable was the face of the thin, sallow man who stood by Virgil Earp. This man wore the dress of a gambler and from under his coat, in a shoulder clip, was a ten gauge, twin barrel shot pistol. His pallid face was set in a cold and mocking grin as he looked on.

"What's the trouble, King?" asked Earp, stepping forward, by the two gunmen and halting at Rambeau's side. His eyes turned to Frank Leslie, glanced at the three cowhands then he snapped, "Making trouble again, Leslie?"

"This's private," Leslie replied. "Go peddle for votes some other place."

"Leave this to me, King," Earp said grimly, satisfied that his brother and Doc Holliday were on hand and that he had a good audience. "I can handle it."

Rambeau moved back a pace, his hand still hovering his gun. He hated Leslie both as a man and a business rival and this would be a good chance to force the play. Never would he have a better chance, two men of his own, Wyatt and Virgil Earp and Doc Holliday against Leslie and two cowhands, three if a man troubled to count that small runt on the big paint horse.

"Leslie," Earp began. "I'm getting——"

"Mr. Earp," Dusty cut in with an easy, gentle drawl. "You remember a skinhunter in Dodge, name of Shag Moxel?—— I'm the man who killed him."

Earp's face had flushed with annoyance at the interruption to his noble speech. Then the annoyance died and for an instant a flicker of something else took its place. Only for an instant was it there, then the face became an impassive mask again but Dusty had caught the expression. So had Mark, the Kid and Frank Leslie; caught it and read it for what it was.

"He's telling you true, Wyatt," said Doc Holliday from the sidewalk. "I was in town, didn't get called out on business like you and Bat. I saw him right after he did it."

There were times when Wyatt Earp wondered he ever took up with such an out and out ornery cuss as Doc Holliday. One thing Earp did not want was confirmation of the identity of the man who killed Shag Moxel. It still rankled Earp to remember how he'd left town when Dusty Fog came looking for the man who tried to kill his cousin Ben Holland. That was five years ago but Earp remembered every detail of it and so did Doc Holliday.

It was then a whisper ran through the crowd, loud enough for Earp to hear and give confirmation to his knowledge and memory.

"Yes, sir. That's him. The Rio Hondo gun wizard. That's Captain Dusty Fog."

"How're you calling it, Wyatt?" Holliday went on, always

ready to fan up the flames and start the ball rolling.

There was death in the air of Tombstone that morning. It hung there poised and seething, just waiting for the first move to let it have its head. One move, one wrong word and guns would roar, men would die and the town of Tombstone would see its boothill grow.

Virgil Earp came forward but he came with hand away from his guns. He came as a peacemaker and not the kind which Colonel Colt's Hartford factory made so well.

"Break it off, Wyatt. Pull in your horns, King. If Buckskin Frank doesn't want to introduce you to the lady leave it lie. You're not fast enough to set in on a deal against a man like Captain Fog."

It was not clear to the crowd, or to Earp and Rambeau, which of them he meant by this last statement. The words did give Wyatt Earp a chance to get out of a real tight spot. Rambeau's two hired hands showed some relief now for they had a certain reluctance to match Colt courtesies with the four hard-eyed, deadly looking men who faced them.

The only one who showed any sign of making a play was Rambeau, then suddenly he knew that he would not get the backing of the Earps. He knew he would have to back out now or lose their not over-strong friendship. To the Earps Rambeau was a man who could be useful for passing out pro-Law and Order Party talk and for handing over generous sums to the campaign funds. He was nothing beyond that, having neither the gun-speed or ability to make himself a useful backer in any shooting which might be needed.

"All right, Virgil," he said. "Leslie's some touchy. I'll get to know the lady later."

With that Rambeau turned and walked away, followed by his men. Wyatt Earp was next to go, knowing he was leaving the field second best, but satisfied to be leaving it on his feet. Virgil stood for a moment, shrugged, turned and followed his brother.

The tension oozed from the watching crowd but talk rolled up among them. Leslie knew there was nothing more to be gained by standing here and so suggested to Madame Paula that she got her people into the wagon and headed for the rooming house where he'd booked them accommodation.

"Like to thank you for sitting in, Dusty," he said while the show folks climbed back into the wagon.

"Any time, Frank. Any old time," Dusty answered. "Where'd we be likely to find Texas John if he's in town?"

"He came in last night and he'll be in my place later. Go down and wait for him. I'll be along after I've seen my folks bedded down."

The two groups separated, Dusty, Mark and the Kid taking their horses to the livery barn and then making for the Bucket of Blood Saloon. They'd just finished making their bets when Texas John Slaughter came in. He was a smallish, tanned, hard looking man dressed in the style of a Texas cowhand, yet about him there was the unmistakable something which told other cowhands that here was a master of their trade.

Dusty came from the bar, holding out his hand which Slaughter gripped in a friendly shake. "Howdy John," Dusty said. "I came as soon as Uncle Devil got your telegraph message."

The rancher shook hands with Mark and the Kid after Dusty and then waved to a nearby table, suggesting they took the weight off their legs and talked things out.

"You know why I sent you?" he asked.

"Only what you said in the telegraph message," Dusty answered. "We've just signed in for the shooting. Though why you wanted us out from Texas just for that I don't know."

"See the boards, how Earp's favoured high for both shoots," drawled Slaughter. "He mustn't win either of them. If he does Tombstone and Cochise County'll toss their votes his way when they come to elect their sheriff. Then we'll be under Kansas lawmen and you know what that means."

"I wouldn't wish that on a carpet-bagging Republican," drawled Mark grimly.

"Was I a praying man I'd say amen to that," went on the Kid.

Kansas lawmen. They were an anathema to any Texas cowhand who'd trailed a herd north to the railheads. The men who ran the law in the trail end towns were for the most part northern sympathisers with a built-in hatred for those rebel Texas boys who came with the cattle. The hatreds of the Civil War were fanned afresh by the men who wore the badges of town marshal, kept alight by the way they treated the cowhands. To every Texan a Kansas lawman was a cold-blooded cowardly murderer at worst or a bribe taking pimp at best. Wyatt Earp's name ranked high on the list of Kansas lawmen and for him to run the law in Cochise County would mean bloodshed.

"Earp's after the sheriff's post then?" asked Dusty.

"Pushing all he can, him and the rest of the Law and Order Party. I wouldn't take sides, Dusty, but he's been boasting so loud and long I reckon it's time his bet was called."

"And you reckon we can stop him winning?" asked Dusty with a smile.

"Reckon?" scoffed Slaughter. "I'd be tolerable surprised if you couldn't."

While the men were talking, Buckskin Frank Leslie entered the saloon, having seen his people safely to their accommodation. He passed the table without more than a friendly greeting for a sudden thought had struck him while delivering Madame Paula. It was a thought which caused him to make a hurried and apologetic departure without even waiting for Joe Raymond to finish his unpacking and come for a drink.

The bartender laid aside the cloth with which he was polishing the glasses and came along to greet the boss, grinning broadly and jerking a thumb to the table.

"Those cowhands throw their money around," he said jovially, sure his boss was going to be pleased with his making money for the business. "Signed on for the shooting in the Fair. I set the two tall ones in at three to one, I didn't want to offend them by going any higher. The dark boy's took it to win on the rifle and the blond to come in second or third with the revolvers."

"Three to one?" gurgled Leslie, thankful the saloon had not been full of men who knew the West.

"Sure," grinned the bartender. "The best laugh was when that little feller took on for the Pistol Match."

Somehow, the bartender thought, the joke was falling flat. He could not think how or why. There was a look of horror almost on Leslie's usually expressionless face, for he was not looking at the bartender, but at the board on which the odds were written.

"Ten to one!" The words were torn from Leslie as if every

one of them hurt him. "You laid odds of ten to one that *Dusty Fog* didn't win the Match?" He shot out a hand across the bar. "Give me that rag and chalk, quick!"

At the table John Slaughter was staring at Mark Counter in amazement.

"Ten to one, Mark?" he gasped. "You're jobbing me."

Mark grinned broadly for he was seated facing the bar and watching Leslie's agitated actions. "Was I never to leave this chair again, John, I'm telling you the bartender started Dusty at ten to one. I stand at three to one for a place and he put Lon in at three to one for a win with his old yellow boy."

Money jingled in Slaughter's pocket as he thrust back his chair. He could not see what was happening at the bar.

"I always thought you didn't gamble, John," drawled Dusty casually.

"So who's gambling? It's like finding money in the street."

For all that John Slaughter was cautious as he crossed the room, heading for the bar. He did not glance at the boards but leaned by Leslie, who was standing also with his back to the boards, looking just as relaxed and unconcerned.

"Fine day, Frank," Slaughter said.

"Real fine," agreed Leslie.

"They do tell me Dusty there's in for the Pistol Match at the Fair," Slaughter went on. "I reckon I might have a couple of dollars on him just for old time's sake."

With that Slaughter leaned back and offered Leslie a cigar. They were friends or the rancher would never have thought of playing things this way. It would make a good story to say he'd got the better of Frank Leslie and taken odds of ten to one that Dusty Fog did not win the shooting match. However, it had to be played careful or Leslie might see the board in time and alter the odds to something more in keeping, as would be his right.

"Yes, sir," Slaughter went on in the nonchalant, disinterested tone of a horse-trader trying to get a hundred dollar stallion for the price of a wind-broken plug. "Just lay this here two dollars on Dusty Fog for me, barkeep."

Slaughter offered the money, still without looking at the board and took the slip in return. Then he turned, a broad grin spreading on his face—and dying again.

"What the——!"

Leslie had made good with his time. Dusty Fog's name was still there but the odds showed a thick broad white mark where other writing had been erased. Now they stood not at ten to one, but at even money.

"Reckon the drinks are on you, John," Dusty remarked, coming to the bar.

"You saw what he was doing and never said a word," replied Slaughter. "Let me go against my principles and start betting——"

"You reckon you've worries," answered Leslie with a grin. "How about me if the place had been full? It's nothing but luck that nobody got any money down."

"I wouldn't go so far as to say that," drawled Mark as he and the Kid joined the others. "Nope, I wouldn't say that at all."

With that Mark held the receipt so that Leslie could see it and read the amount on it. Leslie shrugged. One bet wouldn't break—then he saw the Kid also held out a slip.

"No." The word came in a strangled gasp. "Hank, you didn't take these bets, did you? You did? Oh well, we might break even on the bets we've got on already."

The Kid grinned and held out his receipt. "Is she worth fifty dollars as she stands, Frank?"

"Any time, right now if you like."

"Here, barkeep," laughed the Kid. "Throw this away and make it out at the right odds. Man, your face when you saw it, Frank."

Mark and the Kid exchanged their betting slips, giving away odds of ten to one without a thought. Buckskin Frank Leslie was their friend and they would not take advantage of the slip.

"Say, who was that handsome dude out there on the street?" Dusty asked.

"King Rambeau," Leslie replied. "He runs the King Saloon for the syndicate. Got him one of their top guns on hand, Iowa Parsons."

Dusty sipped at his beer thoughtfully. The syndicate were the unknown group who ran saloons, gambling houses and dance halls throughout Arizona. They controlled at least one place in every town and their take must have been high. Dusty was curious, the handsome saloon owner was not the usual type of man the syndicate put in charge of their places.

"Where's he from?" he asked.

"Ran a place in New York until he had to buy a trunk and head West. There's some talk that he's trying to work a private move, without the syndicate, although I don't know what it is. They shipped him Parsons in when Billy Clanton allowed he'd been cold-decked and it looked like trouble. Parsons has been here ever since."

Mark glanced in the mirror. He was rather more dishevelled than he cared to appear in public so he cut in before Dusty could ask any more about King Rambeau.

"I'm going for a haircut and bath," he said. "Then we can go and show the ladies of Tombstone what they don't have to go on missing."

"We'll come along, Mark," Dusty answered. "See you back here, John. What do you want us to do from now on until the Fair starts?"

"Come out to my place if you like," Slaughter replied. "Leave it until you're freshed up. We'll have a night in town and then see what you reckon."

"That sits well with us," Dusty answered. "We'll see you later then."

Slaughter and Leslie watched the three young Texans leave the saloon and the rancher grinned. "Now there goes the three best men I know."

Leslie crumpled the two betting receipts in his palm and tossed them into a spittoon. "You're right about that, John," he replied.

CHAPTER FOUR

King Rambeau Makes Demands

Dusty Fog walked with his two friends along Toughnut Street, making for the barber's shop Leslie recommended to him. He thought as he looked around that these wide-open towns were much the same. The faces changed but the general type of people remained the same. The same sort of crowds moved along the sidewalks, the same type of business premises flourished. There were mine workers, burly men with sleeves rolled up to expose their biceps and strong arms, with levis trousers that had the seam stitching reinforced with brass clips and with steel toed boots. There were cowhands with wide-brimmed Stetson hats worn at just the right "jack-deuce" angle, over the offside eye, gay shirts and levis with cuffs turned back. There were towns-men of various types, the better class in good broadcloth suits, the others in lesser grades of suiting. Mingled among this crowd were drummers, salesmen in loud check suits and derby hats, and cavalrymen on furlough.

All in all the scene was one of constant change, of colour and what appeared to be unending numbers. It was Tombstone but it might just as well have been Dodge City, Quiet Town, Mulrooney or any of the other towns which boomed wild, woolly and wide open, then faded and were gone.

"Man, Tombstone's surely grown some since we were here last," drawled the Kid, watching the passing crowd as they strolled along.

"It's just like Dodge, Newton, Wichita or any of the big trail end towns when the herds were in and the crews paid off," Mark replied, giving a wink at a pretty young girl who smiled, then turned her sunbonneted head away as her mother gave an angry snort.

"More like Quiet Town," said Dusty with a smile, for he'd noticed the wink and its result. "There were never any mine workers in the trail end towns."

"Quiet Town," the Kid remarked. "Now there was a town. She was the wildest of them all."

Dusty could have agreed with that. Quiet Town, in Montana, and just after the War had been the wildest of them all. It had also been the first town in which he held the law badge and it was the first town he tamed, with the aid of his tough and handy deputies.

On a quiet side street they found the building they were looking for. It was a long, fairly new looking building and split into three parts. The first window had a display of male clothing, clothing to suit the cowhand, the mine worker, the town dweller or the professional gambler. Next door to this was the barber's shop and beyond it the bath house. This was an ideal arrangement and showed some considerable forethought on the part of its owner. It was situated handily to the edge of town and the men coming in from the mines or the ranches could enter one building, take a bath, then have shave and haircut and finally spend money on a change of clothing before going on to the pleasures of the town.

The barber's shop was crowded when Dusty and Mark emerged from the bathroom. They'd been before the Kid in the baths and so were ready for their haircuts while he was still soaking in the hot water. All three of the chairs were occupied and the barbers working fast while the lather boy attended to his stove kettle and worked up lather. In the seats around the walls sat the other customers, there were only two spaces left, one on either side of the street door of the building. Dusty took one and Mark the other, sitting back and listening to the conversation, the jokes and small talk which flashed between the barbers and the customers.

Time passed and a customer left the chair to allow the next man in. A tall, tanned, spare man in his early thirties rose to take a vacant chair. Dusty looked the man over, noting he wore cowhand dress of a style which showed he had money to spare, and was probably a rancher. There was something more about him, he walked with the stride of a horseman, but did not have that something which marked the born and bred cowhand. He did not wear a gunbelt either and that was strange; it was almost like seeing a man without his trousers, fact being there were men in Tombstone who might forget their trousers when rising in the morning—but they would never forget to strap on their guns.

The tall man was almost at the chair when the door of the shop opened and three men entered. One moved towards the vacant chair, the other two stopped with their shoulders against the door, their hands thumb-hooked into their gunbelts near the butts of the low-tied Colts.

Dusty had a good memory for faces and recognised the newcomers. They were Mr. Earp's friend, King Rambeau, and his two gunmen. More, they were clearly looking for trouble with the tall man who was next in line for a haircut. Dusty glanced by the two gunmen and caught Mark's eye. By the slight inclination of Mark's head Dusty knew he was not alone in the recognition and was set for trouble.

"Just a minute, Brownlow," Rambeau said, dropping his hand to the back of the chair and turning it from the other man. "I've been looking for you. Haven't seen you for a couple of days."

The man called Brownlow's eyes met Rambeau's for a long moment. "That could be because I saw you first each time."

Dusty looked harder at Brownlow. He recognized the accent and it was not American. Those clipped, decisive and firm tones were British and upper-class British at that. Dusty had met some of these British gentlemen who had come West to find excitement and a new life. They were just what the word said, gentlemen in the strictest sense. He liked and admired their kind, it was their drive and spirit which made England the great country it was.

There was no hint of a smile on Rambeau's face and he kept his hand on the chair back, never taking his eyes from the other man's face. All talk in the shop had died down now, every eye on the two men. The barber, the burly owner of the building, drew back from his chair.

"Have you thought over my offer?" Rambeau asked.

"It didn't need thinking about. I'll take the chair and have my haircut."

"Not yet. I'm in a hurry and I want the chair."

"'Fraid not," replied Brownlow. "I've waited my turn and so can you."

With that the man gripped the chair and turned it back towards him but before he could sit down Rambeau had kicked it so it spun back towards him once more.

"You don't get a haircut today or any other day, Brownlow. Not unless you cut me in on that herd."

There was no fear in Brownlow's face, only a slight tightening of his lips as he replied, "Do you run Tombstone now?"

"You haven't been able to hire a hand, have you?"

"I put that down more to your hired killer than to any effort on your part," Brownlow replied and his voice grew hard. "Move your foot and I'll have the chair."

Rambeau grinned, showing his coat clear of the gun butt. "I'm having it. Are you fixing to stop me?"

The watching men were silent. Not a Tombstone dweller here but who knew what was going on between Rambeau and the tall Englishman. There had been word passing around the town that no cowhand had better take on to drive cattle for Vance Brownlow on pain of offending Iowa Parsons, boss gun for King Rambeau. Why this was, not one man present, apart from the two main actors of the scene, could say. One thing was for sure, whatever their differences King Rambeau was now forcing the issue. The two gunhung men at the door would prevent anyone either going to fetch the law, or help Brownlow.

Rambeau's foot came down from the chair and he moved back a pace his hand lifting to hover his gun butt. Dusty watched the other man, saw how his feet moved slightly into what could have been a fighting stance. Dusty noticed the way the man stood but more so at the way the right fist was held. The hand was closed but the fist knuckle extended beyond the others in what at first might have appeared an awkward manner. Dusty's brows drew together in a puzzled frown. Either the Englishman did not know anything much about defending himself with his hands, or he knew a very effective way.

"Make your choice," Rambeau sneered. "I'm either your partner and you can have the chair. Or I'm not and we settle it right now."

"On your terms, you armed and I'm not?"

Never taking his eyes from Brownlow the handsome saloon-keeper spoke to the owner of the shop:

"Barber, take one of your customer's guns and put it on the chair in front of Brownlow. I'll give him a chance."

The barber gulped. He knew something about guns and shooting and knew Vance Brownlow would have no chance in a fight, not like that. He would have to bend for the gun, straighten and line it. With a strange gun in his hand he would have no chance at all. The only difference would be that Brownlow would be armed, technically, and so Rambeau could plead self-defence.

"I'm waiting, barber," Rambeau went on. "You've got a real nice place here. You wouldn't want anything to happen to it, now would you?"

That showed the barber clearly where he stood. He must do as Rambeau demanded or his business would suffer for it. Rambeau worked for the syndicate, that was a common piece of knowledge around town, and the syndicate knew every method for making life uncomfortable for people who crossed them. He looked at the other customers of his shop, then at Brownlow, and licked his lips nervously.

Dusty Fog's right foot tapped on the floor in a casual and what might have been taken for a nervous gesture. Mark Counter caught the sign and just slightly tensed, ready for the sudden action he knew was coming.

Faster than a striking rattlesnake and with much less warning Dusty made his move. His right hand lashed out and back suddenly. The way the hand was held looked strange to a man used to seeing fist fighters in action. Instead of clenching the fist Dusty kept his fingers extended, held together with the thumb over his palm. The hand, edge sideways, lashed around, aimed with skill and precision straight for the gunman's solar plexus. The gunman caught the first move from Dusty and dropped his hand towards his gun. He was a full half-second too late for the blow landed before the gun was clear. Awkward though the way Dusty struck appeared to the gunman the blow came like the bite of the edge of an axe. His hand missed the butt of his gun as he gave a croaking gasp and doubled forward, the breath forced from his lungs in a painful manner. Gasping in pain the man sank to his knees, his face an ashy grey colour and masked with agony.

The second gunman started to grab for his gun and almost made it. Fingers which gripped like the closing jaws of a bear trap clamped on to his arm. He gave what started as an angry curse and ended as a yell of agony as his wrist was crushed in powerful hands. Mark Counter came to his feet, swinging the gunman before him with no more trouble than if he was handling a baby. Then Mark brought the gunman's arm up behind his back. The man was bent forward, helpless in those hands. Mark turned again until they faced the wall. Then with a sudden surge of his muscles Mark sent the man hurling head first into the wall. The gunman's head hit hard and with a moan of pain he sank down.

Rambeau saw, reflected in the mirror, what was happening to his men. He started to swing around with his hand dropping and lifting his gun. He recognized Dusty and Mark as the two men who had backed Leslie on the street and once more they had crossed his path.

For all his gunfighter's belt Rambeau was not fast with his gun. The Colt was lifting as Dusty came to his feet, right hand flickering across his body. Yet from so far behind Dusty still had his gun out and lined before Rambeau cleared leather. The bone handled Colt was in Dusty's hand, the left holster empty, the hammer drawn back under his thumb and the four and three-quarter-inch barrel lined on Rambeau's middle froze the saloon-keeper's draw still not more than half done.

"Don't try it, Rambeau," warned Dusty.

It was at that moment Rambeau realised what Iowa Parsons had told him all the time since he bought the gunbelt. Parsons' off-repeated warning that Rambeau was not fast enough to tote a gun in such a rig was clear now. The saloon-keeper had come West after his saloon on New York's Bowery had grown too hot for comfort. He had come from a world where a gun was not yet considered as a useful tool for settling a difference and had started to learn, too late, the secrets of handling a smoking Colt in a Western corpse-and-cartridge affair. Slowly his hand came away from his gun and for the first time in his life he knew the raw ache of fear biting into him. He swore that never again would he be fool enough to strap on a gunbelt.

"I'll take the chair, Rambeau," Brownlow said coolly.

That put the play back in Rambeau's hands once more but he no longer fancied backing it. Without being told he knew murder was out, even murder done under the flimsy guise of self-defence. That small—small? Suddenly Dusty Fog was small no more in Rambeau's eyes, in fact he suddenly appeared to tower taller than any other man in the room to the saloon-keeper. That fast-moving Texan would never allow Rambeau to call the play with guns.

There was the prospect of standing up against Vance Brownlow in a rough-house brawl but no longer was that appealing to Rambeau. He was a skilled fist fighter who learned his game in the slums of New York but the Britisher was also skilled and his ways of fighting were something completely beyond Rambeau's understanding. He did not wish to get into a fight and risk having his handsome face marked up. Not when he thought of that beautiful young actress who arrived in town that morning. Rambeau was proud of his good looks and did not want them marked. Marked they would get if he stacked up against Vance Brownlow.

"I'll not forget this, Brownlow," he snarled, turning to cross the room to where Dusty's victim was getting to his feet, groaning and holding his stomach. He looked back at Vance Brownlow and went on, "You've done wrong, hiring a gun."

"I never saw either of these gentlemen before," Vance Brownlow replied. "I'm sorry, chappie, but I don't need a partner. Much less do I need one who puts nothing in and wants to take twenty-five per cent of all the profits out."

With that the tall Englishman sat in the chair in a gesture which clearly showed the interview was over as far as he was concerned. Rambeau's face showed anger but he kept clear his hand from the gun butt. Dusty Fogg stood to one side, his Colt back in the holster but that meant nothing as Rambeau knew. It had been in the holster before, but came out fast enough. Rambeau turned his anger on the gunman who was now on his feet.

"Get your pard up," he snarled, jerking a thumb towards the groaning man on the floor. "Let's get out of here."

The gunman gritted his teeth but bent and helped the other man to his feet. Rambeau jerked open the door and the two gunmen went by him; he stood for an instant, then turned and left, slamming the door behind him. The customers let out their breath in a long and concerted sigh which was echoed by the three barbers and the lather boy. This latter had stood from start to finish holding the lather-brush poised in the air.

"Excuse me, mister," said the prosperous-looking townsman who had been seated by Mark, rising to look at Dusty. "No offence meant, but I was wondering if you had entered for the pistol shoot?"

The man spoke with some care. It paid to do so when addressing such a remark to a man who wore two guns in a rig like that with the holster bottoms tied down. It was a saying in the West that a man who tied down his holster bottom was apt not to talk much with his mouth.

"Reckon I am, sir," Dusty answered.

"Wouldn't take it wrong was I to ask your name, mister?" the man went on in a polite and respectful tone. "I'd surely admire to lay a bet on you."

"No offence taken. The name's Dusty Fog."

"Dusty Fog!" the well-dressed man's repeating of Dusty's name was echoed by every other man in the shop. "I'll be back in a minute, Sid!"

The same idea apparently struck every other customer in the shop, including the two who were receiving treatment in the chair. There was a sudden rush for the door and Tombstone was presented with the spectacle of several citizens, including one with one side of his hair short, the other long and shaggy and the other with half his face still lathered, the barber's towels still around their necks, heading at a dead run for the Bucket of Blood Saloon.

Dusty watched the exit, then turned and grinned to the

barber, who was by the cash drawer and taking money out.

"I'm sorry we cost you some trade, friend," he said.

"That kind of gunwork don't need no apologising for, Cap'n Fog," replied the owner of the shop. Then he turned to the lather boy. "Sammywell," he said, holding out the money, "head for the Bucket of Blood and ask the bartender to put this on Cap'n Fog in the Pistol Shoot."

The lather boy took the money and the other two barbers also handed over bets to be placed for them. The lather boy left the shop on the run and the barber waved a hand to the now empty chairs. A grin came to his face as he thought of the chance he had to win, for he was betting on Iowa Parsons and Wyatt Earp as well. Now it looked as if he'd covered all the bets.

"Take a seat, gents," the barber said. "Looks like you won't have to wait at all."

The Kid emerged from the bathroom and took a seat. He did not know what had happened, but was pleased to see he would not have to wait long for his haircut. His two friends and another man appeared to be the only customers and they were in the chairs now.

Vance Brownlow looked across to the two cowhands as they sat back, the towels in place and the barber's shears moving.

"I haven't thanked you two gentlemen yet," he said. "I hope you will allow me to show my appreciation by standing you a meal at the Eating House when we're done."

"No thanks are needed, friend," Dusty replied.

"I was watching how you hit that gunman, Captain Fog," Brownlow went on. "It's a remarkable coincidence but you used something like a karate trick I learned from a Japanese merchant in Hong Kong. I was a young subaltern in the Rifles out there."

"Now that's a real coincidence," Dusty answered and his two friends grinned as they listened. "I thought I was using the *tegatana* against his *suigetsu*."

"Gad!" Vance Brownlow ejaculated, twisting around in the chair and looking at Dusty with more interest. "I could have sworn that I was the only man in Arizona knew karate."

Dusty chuckled. "You'd best sit back afore you leave an ear on the floor. I learned karate and ju-jitsu down home to the Rio Hondo country. My Uncle Devil's man Tommy Akasi, taught me. I didn't know if the handsword would work against his solar plexus, but I reckon it did."

Vance Brownlow threw back his head and laughed, making the barber jerk back his clippers in a hurry to avoid cutting the rancher's head.

"I think it did at that. I hope you accept my offer of the meal down at Mother Handy's place."

"We never refused a meal yet," Dusty replied. "It's on your head though. Your friends'll likely cut you dead if they see you in the street, associating with folks like us."

Before the other customers returned Dusty, Mark and Brownlow were finished and the Ysabel Kid sat having his long black hair trimmed.

CHAPTER FIVE

Vance Brownlow Needs Hands

Mother Handy's eating house stood on Toughnut Street, a large, white painted wooden building, clean looking and giving forth appetising smells which boded well for the meals served on the inside.

There was a good crowd in the Eating House when Vance Brownlow entered with the three Texans. He led them to a table by the central aisle and they sat around it, hanging their hats on the backs of the chairs. The waitresses, three pretty girls in black dresses and clean white aprons, moved among the other customers and did not give Brownlow's party a glance. At the door of the kitchen Mother Handy, a smallish, plump and white-haired old woman, neatly dressed, gentle in appearance, was giving the cook the benefit of a tongue lashing that did not fit in with her appearance at all. She turned, slammed the door and came down the aisle to halt by Brownlow's table, smiled at the men as they shoved back their chairs and started to rise.

"Sit down, all of ye," she said. "Vance, me darlin' boy,

and when is it you'll be bringing us some of that good beef in?"

No question need ever be asked to Mother Handy's home country, not with a brogue thicker than a New York Irish policeman's on Saint Patrick's Day.

"As soon as I can gather in a trail crew," Vance replied, without looking at his guests. "Birdie's trying around town right now."

"Huh!" snorted Mother Handy. "I've been hearing why it is you can't get the men." Her eyes went to Dusty Fog, Mark Counter and the Ysabel Kid. For a moment she studied the Kid's Indian dark face, then she nodded. If three men like these, so obviously tophands, had taken on to ride for Vance Brownlow, he would get all the others he needed. She asked no questions, that was never done. "I can't offer you much by the way of meat, boys. The Folks in town are eating it faster than the local ranchers can supply it."

"Never heard tell that the Clantons or the McLowery boys had trouble raising beef, ma'am," drawled the Kid. "They do tell that every Clanton cow has at least five calves and even some of the bulls have young 'uns too."

"Well, I wouldn't buy nothing from the likes of them. I can prove all the beef I buy isn't stolen. I wouldn't buy no kind of dishonest goods."

"Smuggled wine isn't dishonest then, ma'am?" asked the Kid mildly.

The old woman snorted explosively, the sudden annoyance came and left her face as she laughed, holding out her hand to the Kid. "Lon Ysabel," she gasped. "The Saints preserve us. I heard you'd been killed down in Mexico just after the War. Sure and you're not still doing that awful and evil smuggling, now are you?"

For all the outburst there was a note which was more of hope than condemnation in the old woman's voice as she looked at the boy, who, with his father, had sold her more than one consignment of good wine on which no duty ever was paid to the U.S. Customs.

"Nope, I done retired," the Kid answered sadly.

The old woman opened her mouth to make a suggestion to

Vance, then closed it again. She took their order for the meal, turned and headed for the kitchen to roust up the cook. Mother Handy liked Vance Brownlow and his pretty wife and hoped they would be able to get the men they needed. However, she could not interfere in their private business. If Vance had hired the three Texans all would be well. If he had not, Mother Handy could hardly poke her nose in and interfere.

"Would a man be out of line to ask what's between you and Rambeau?" Mark asked of Vance after the old woman walked away.

Before the question could be answered there was an interruption. The door of the room burst suddenly open and a small, plump yet pretty blonde woman entered and came across to the table. There was anger on her face. There was anger in the way she stamped down her dainty, high-heeled boots. Her white Stetson was thrust back from her head and hung on her back by the storm strap. Her blonde hair was cut short and curly, the hair style a woman living far from other women would choose as being easily cared for and need little attention. Her figure was plump, yet there was hard, firm flesh, not flabby fat. Her round, full breasts strained against the open necked tartan shirt and her hips strained the washed-out blue jeans which hung cowhand style outside her boots.

She halted at Brownlow's table, resting her hands on the top and looking straight at him. "I couldn't raise a single man, Vance boy," she said.

"I didn't think you would."

"I could have if that Iowa Parsons hadn't followed me every place I went," the woman went on angrily, her voice a Texas drawl under the anger.

"Did he say or do anything to you?" Vance snapped angrily and started to thrust back his chair.

"Nope, so pull in your horns. Parsons wouldn't let you get in close enough to get one of those ju-jitsu holds on him."

"This here Iowa Parsons, ma'am," put in Mark, still on his feet, as were the other two Texans, having risen when the woman approached, "they do tell he's a good friend of that nice Mr. Rambeau we're all so fond of and pleased to know."

To give the woman credit, she'd hardly noticed the three

Texans in her annoyance. Now she studied them with eyes which knew cowhands in general and Texas cowhands in particular.

"He does," she snorted. "That fancy dressed, scent-smelling Arbuckle hires Parsons as his boss gun, and meaner, colder, back shooting Yankee sidewinder'd be hard to find, man or boss."

"Way you all get to talking, ma'am," put in the Kid politely and mildly, "a man'd think you didn't like neither of them."

"Don't like them!" the woman's voice rose a shade. "Don't like them. I tell you all. I'd as soon have the Earps, the Republican Party or two skunks settle on me than them pair. Why they make old Carpetbag Davis's dirty State Police look like good and honest Southern gentlemen."

Dusty smiled, a broad smile which was mirrored by the grins of his friends as they took their seats again. The woman was not English, that was for sure. She was as Texas as the Alamo, the Lone Star flag or any of the three young men from Ole Devil Hardin's Rio Hondo outfit. There was no doubting the State she hailed from, not with that accent or her reference to ex-Governor Davis's State Police, a force which had been brought to Texas to replace the Rangers after the War. The State Police had a career which varied from rank incompetence to extortion and robbery instead of one of crime prevention and the Police finally disbanded when Davis was forcibly tossed from office. They were a force for which the average Texan felt nothing but scorn.

"You wouldn't be from Texas, now would you, ma'am?" Dusty asked as he drew out a chair for her to sit down.

"I surely didn't know it showed," she answered, taking the seat and looking at the men. "I've been trying to hide it since I married Vance. Anyways, that King Rambeau'd make a prissy Eastern schoolmarm cuss fit to throw her teeth."

The three men were then introduced to Mrs. Birdie Brownlow and Mark turned his attention back to Vance once more.

"You never got around to telling us about your problem, Vance."

"There's no trouble at all, much. I've got a herd of five hundred head, all prime beef. I want to bring them into Tombstone in time for the County Fair."

"Which same's not much of a problem," drawled the Kid. "Unless there's some more to it."

"There is just a trifle more," Vance agreed. "I was over-simplifying things a trifle. My place is ten days' drive from here, on the other side of the Carne River, which has only one decent crossing we can use to get here on time."

"And there's maybe half the Apache nation just sitting some-wheres between our spread and Tombstone, licking their fat old lips and thinking how good that same herd's going to smell and taste in their stewpot."

"Which same'd make a tolerable large stewpot, taking five hundred head at one go," remarked the Kid.

Birdie game him a cold look and then ignored him. "Trouble being we daren't weaken the ranch crew any to run the herd in," she told the other two, "which's why Vance and I came in a week back. Now Rambeau's sent Parsons out to make sure we don't get the men."

"Why'd he do that, 'cepting for meanness, ma'am?" asked the Kid.

"The price of beef is rising every day. Just before the Fair starts that herd will bring in five—six times as much as it would normally. I know it, so does Rambeau. He came to see me the first day into town and offered to get me all the men I'd need for twenty-five per cent of the gross price of the herd," Vance explained, sensing the others were becoming interested and feeling hope rise.

"Which same's a tolerable fair spread for a man who is running on nothing more than muscle, happen you didn't know," Birdie went on.

"Do tell, ma'am," drawled Mark. "I haven't been around much."

"That I could tell one eyed," she replied.

"Anyway," Vance spoke up, marvelling, as he always did, at the casual and relaxed way in which his wife became friendly with cowhands, "I told Rambeau he'd the wrong chappie and I declined his offer. Then his man, Iowa Parsons, started passing the word he'd kill any man who hired to me."

The Ysabel Kid was seated so he could see the window of the room and through it he saw three men pass by. He saw the shape of one of them at the door and a grin came to his face.

"Do you reckon to be lucky, Vance?" he asked.

Vance Brownlow looked at his wife and smiled. "I think I am."

"You've never been luckier than now," drawled the Kid as the door opened.

The three men who entered were Texas cowhands, top-hands too, if the signs did not lie. In the center was a tall, slim, somehow military looking young man. There was an air of command about him, the look of a man used to giving orders. His clothing was functional cowhand rig, yet expensive, and around his waist was a gunbelt built for speed, with a low tied ivory handled Colt Cavalry Peacemaker in the holster. His face was handsome, or would have been but for the sabre scar which twisted and marked his right cheek.

The other two were cowhands, Texas cowhands at that. Their hats were thrust back and both were red heads, the taller's hair a fiery thatch, the shorter's a rusty mop. The taller was handsome, wide shouldered, lean waisted and tall as the Ysabel Kid. He wore a gunbelt and in the holster at his left side was a staghorn butted Army Colt, one of the old 1860 percussion fired models, but still in a fast draw holster with the tip tied down. The last of the trio was not as tall, he was cheerily good looking, stocky and his low hanging, plain handled Colt was no decoration, even though he did not have the look of a real fast man about him. He was laughing at something one of the others had said, when he came to a halt, the laugh died and a hard expression took its place as he looked towards Brownlow's party.

"Say, Johnny," he said in a cold voice. "It's that Rio Hondo varmint. We owe him some from last time. Don't we?"

"We sure do, Rusty," replied the taller red head. "Let's hand it to him now."

The two men moved forward, their friend standing at the door with a half-smile playing on his lips as he watched them bearing down on Dusty Fog.

For his part, Dusty gave no sign other than to move back his chair so he was free from the table. The two cowhands were approaching, Johnny slightly ahead of Rusty. Then suddenly the taller man's hand lashed out, folded in a fist, at Dusty's head. It was a blow hard enough to drop an ox and would have knocked Dusty clear across the room had it landed.

Dusty left his chair with the speed which had made his name a legend. His hands came up to trap the cowhand's wrist as it whistled towards his head. Jerking the arm upwards over his head, Dusty privoted and turned, bringing the arm down once more. Johnny had no choice but to go over; he gave a yell as his feet left the ground, then he lit down again flat on his back. Rusty let out a yell and tried to get around his friend and into the attack.

Throwing back his chair, Vance started to come to his feet, wondering why Mark and the Kid were not offering to rise and help Dusty. He might also have wondered why two men wearing guns and so obviously able to use them, were fist fighting. Even before Vance could get round the table he was too late.

The cowhand called Johnny lit down on his back. To make sure he did not rise, Dusty moved fast. He released the wrist with one hand, but the other still held the arm stretched out and his foot lifted to stab down with the high heel gouging into Johnny's armpit in a painful manner. With Johnny out of action, Dusty was all set to deal with Rusty's attack.

Rusty's fist drove out right into Dusty's gripping hand. Dusty's thumb bit down on the spot just below the joining of the first and second fingers, on the nerve centers. Rusty gave a squawking yell, his arm was twisted until he was turned and Dusty held it bent up his back. Then Dusty hooked his foot between Rusty's leg and shoved him. Rusty gave a yell and went sprawling at the feet of the tall, scar-faced man. Looking down, the scar-faced man asked, "Don't you ever learn?"

Vance stood with his fists clenched, not knowing what was happening. He saw the Kid lean forward and look at the agonised face of Johnny and ask, "What you doing down there, Johnny?"

The red head managed a grin. "I'm good now, Dusty. Get your foot off'n me."

Mother Handy had emerged from the kitchen with a broom gripped in both hands when she heard the noise, but she could see there was nothing worse than cowhand high spirits, for Dusty was helping Johnny to his feet and the other two men were coming forward with grins on their faces.

"I sure figured we'd got you made there, Dusty," Johnny

remarked, rubbing his hip. "Which same only goes to show, now don't it?"

Vance Brownlow stood still on his feet as the three new-comers began noisy and cheery greetings, shaking hands with Dusty, Mark and the Kid, demanding to know about friends and not waiting for any answer. At last Vance could not longer restrain his curiosity.

"Will somebody tell me what in the name of Sam Hill is going on?"

Dusty took a seat, sliding along to make room for Rusty and Johnny, who were bringing chairs from another table. The talk died down and Dusty gave a laughing answer:

"Vance, Birdie, meet Stone Hart, boss of the Wedge and two of his worthless hands, Johnny Raybold and Rusty Willis."

"The Wedge?" Vance repeated as he looked at the scar-faced young man whose name was spoken of as being one of the finest trail bosses alive. Then Vance remembered the Kid's remark about being lucky and guessed what the words meant.

"I'll take two of your specials, ma'am," said Johnny Raybold, the Wedge's scout, as Mother Handy came alongside them.

"How about your friends?" she answered.

"They'd be tougher than old leather to eat," Johnny drawled. "I'll just take two specials and apple pie to follow."

"Two is it?" yelped Mother Handy indignantly. "No man living can eat two of my specials hand-sitting."

"You wouldn't want to bet on that, would you, ma'am?" asked Rusty Willis eagerly.

"That I would not. But I'll make this agreement with you. If he eats the two specials I'll give him them free. If he doesn't I'll bend my broom over his head."

"She'll do it too, Johnny," warned Birdie.

"I'll just bet she will at that, ma'am," answered Johnny without sounding unduly worried. "Do I get the pie free to follow?"

The old woman gave Johnny a long stare of amazement, snorted and headed for the kitchen to make sure her always well-filled plates were piled up extra high to teach the red-headed upstart a lesson he'd never forget.

"You're a mite off your home range, Stone," the Kid drawled

as they finished their meals and waited for Johnny to wade through his.

"Sure. We were offered a herd to drive for an outfit near here. The Clantons. So I brought the boys along and came down here. We should have been back in town for the Fair, old Chow's entered his chuckwagon for the race. Anyway, I decided not to take the herd on."

"Wouldn't want to be out 'n' out nosey," drawled the Kid, "and ask why—why?"

"Their earmark's what'd be called a grub on the near and a sharp on the off. Then for brands they kind of go in for variety. Mexican maps and greaser madhouses and all from different herds. With that kind of a herd a man's likely to wind up wearing a hemp bandanna at the cottonwood hoe-down."

Stone Hart did not need to explain the words to the others. Grub and sharp earmarks were rarely used on cattle. They were special ways of cutting an animal's ear, brutal and cruel, but little used in the normal line of cattle business. The grub was made by cutting both an under and over slope and left little of an ear to the animal. The sharp was done by cropping the ear to a short point, like that of a boxer dog. Both the earmarks had merit only to a man who wanted to remove the traces of previous and more legitimate earmarks from his cattle. Mexican maps and greaser madhouses were the terms given to the large and complicated brands the ranchers south of the border used on their herds. The Clantons' herd consisted of cattle branded with a variety of such brands, pointing that they came from different herds and were most likely stolen. For a man to be caught driving a stolen herd could bring him a hemp bandanna at a cotton wood hoe-down, or in plain and unvarnished English, to a hanging as guest of honour.

"Those Clantons will go too far one of these days," Vance remarked.

"You're not riding with anybody then, Stone?" Birdie put in eagerly. She was more concerned with getting their herd to Tombstone than with the possible end of the Clantons.

"No, ma'am, we're not."

For an instant Birdie was startled by the brusque way Stone replied and the way he did not, had not since he sat at the table, looked straight at her. She felt annoyed for a moment, then the annoyance died away. Stone Hart was seated so the un-scarred side of his face was towards her. It was a handsome face and the scar was not as bad as he apparently thought. She realised that he must feel bitterly about it and would have liked to tell him that it was not so bad as he imagined, but common sense held her tongue. She knew he would resent bitterly any words about his disfigurement from a stranger.

"Would you care to handle a drive for me, old chap?" Vance asked, catching on to his wife's idea. "A small herd, five hundred head, A hundred miles or so to town and a few hundred Apaches waiting to stop us. I'll pay double the normal rate if you will."

"Pay us the normal rate," Stone answered with a grin. "I'm no Yankee to gouge a man when he's in a tight. Are you riding, Dusty?"

"I'm here for Uncle Devil, doing something for Texas John," Dusty replied. "I'd sure like to ride with you, *amigo,* but I'll have to see how he wants things playing first."

"How about you, Kid?" Stone went on, turning to the Kid. "Johnny's a fair scout, but he's always worked against Northern Indians and not against Apaches. I could use an extra scout."

"I'll ride if Dusty can spare me," replied the Kid. The thought of Apaches and danger never troubled him. He hoped to get a chance to ride with his good friends of the Wedge once more.

"Let's leave her lie on how Texas John wants us, Lon," Dusty suggested. "If you get a full crew, Stone, and we're free, we'll come along for the ride."

"Where's Doc and Waggles and the rest of the crew, Stone?" Mark asked.

"Made camp on a stream outside town. They allow it'll be cheaper than buying a hotel room."

"We'll go out there if you like," Vance suggested. "As soon as Johnny finishes eating. You're the trail boss, Stone. I'll take you out to my ranch, then lend a hand on the way in. Birdie won't stay in town now, or back at the ranch, so she can lend the cook a hand."

There were startled expressions on the faces of the Texas men as they looked at Vance. He wondered what he'd said to bring about such a change in them. He was soon to learn that

Stone Hart's old cook, Chow Willicka, lived by two beliefs.
The first was that no woman ever born, even his own mother,
knew how to cook. The other belief was that women's cooking
would plumb soon ruin a man's innards.

Birdie did not need to be told this, she'd heard cowhands
talk of Chow Willicka, who was acknowledged a master of his
trade. She knew his beliefs and decided to place a dainty and
ladylike foot on them right now from the start.

"You can just set in and tell that fool old chow-spoiler he's
going to have him a reallive female lady louse helping him on
this trip," she warned Stone. "And if he objects or gives me
sass I'll ram his biggest skillet so hard on to his head that his
corns'll be pushed out of his boot soles."

The men all chuckled at the spirited words. They could see
there would be stirring times around the camp fires on the drive
when Chow Willicka and Birdie locked horns. The Kid was
hoping they would be given a chance to ride with the Wedge
if only to see the fun.

"How many will you need, Stone?" Vance asked.

"Normally I'd take a herd that size with just my regular
crew, but with the Apaches out I'd like to take on a few, say
four or five more riders. If that suits you."

"My dear chap, you're the boss. I'm just curious and interested," Vance replied and looked for Mother Handy, waving
for the bill to be brought.

The old woman came to the table and found that Johnny's
two plates were empty and that he was just finishing the last
of the enormous slab of apple pie. He hardly showed any sign
of consuming a meal which would have foundered many a
man.

"I don't believe it," she gasped. "I just don't believe it.
That boy must be all stomach, clean down to his feet."

The others all laughed, although the Texans were far from
surprised at Johnny and his capacity for putting away food.
Mother Handy joined the many other cooks who noted Johnny's
trim figure and thought they could outfeed him. It was a thought
which had saved Johnny more than a few dollars in eating
houses from Texas to Kansas along the cattle trails.

"The boys'll be pleased, Stone," Rusty remarked. "Ole
Peaceful allowed we'd all get into trouble and young Rin's

been trying to borrow money to whup the tail off Buckskin
Frank Leslie's tiger. They'll be right happy to get away from
temptation, especially as they haven't much money left and
the Fair's a fortnight off."

Deep down Stone agreed with Rusty. The failure to take
the Clanton's herd had left his crew short of money and they
would either have to head back to Texas or get work locally
to raise money for the festivities. This way they would be away
until just before the Fair and would pay off, have money in
their pockets.

Vance paid the bill and came to his feet, the others taking
their hats and also rising. Dusty meant to look around and find
Slaughter, learn what the rancher wanted him to do. With that
knowledge he could plan his future, whether to ride with Stone
Hart and Vance or not.

The door of the room was suddenly kicked open and a man
stepped in. Two more followed him, moving like wolves flanking an unstrung buffalo. The two men were hired killers, cheap,
expendable, loyal only as long as the pay was good and the
stakes did not rise too high.

The other man was also a hired killer, but as far above the
others as the ace is over the deuce in a high hand poker game.
He wore a flat-topped black hat, a city shirt and vest, across
which stretched a gold watch chain. His trousers and shoes
equally pointed to the city, but that gunbelt was Western. It
hung just right and told a grim story to a man who knew the
signs as well as Dusty Fog did. That was a fast man's holster,
but so was Dusty's, Mark's and, to a lesser degree, the holsters
of the Ysabel Kid or the three Wedge hands. No, it was more
than just the belt and holster. It was the gun and the way the
holster hung. The leather of the holster was cut to a minimum,
half the chamber, all the trigger-guard and the butt left clear
and just right for an easy reach. The checking of the hammer
tip had been filed off, leaving the spur so that it would slip
free of the thumb easily. The gun and holster hung so the tip
slanted forward and the butt of the gun looked too far back to
a man who knew a little more about such things.

Dusty Fog knew more than a little about guns and holsters.
That method was known as the walk and draw, it was favoured
by professional town laymen who rarely, if ever, rode a horse

and did not need to bother about their guns jarring from the holster while riding. It all spelled one thing to Dusty. This lean, gaunt, dark faced man was a professional and fast—real fast.

"Dusty!" Vance Brownlow gasped as he felt Birdie grip his arm. His voice was no more than a whisper, as if he was mesmerised by that grim faced man before them. "That's Iowa Parsons."

"They say if any man can lick Wyatt Earp in the Fair's Pistol Shoot he's the one who'll do it," Birdie went on. "He's come to stop you hiring to us."

CHAPTER SIX

Shootout at Mother Handy's

The gaunt man called Iowa Parsons stood in the center of the doorway, clearly blocking all exit, the two men flanking him making sure no one could slip by. Word had been brought to them that men were sitting in friendship and might be taking on to drive cattle for Vance Brownlow, and so they came along to lend their skill and backing to the man from the Syndicate, Iowa Parsons.

For a long moment Iowa Parsons studied each of the faces before him, reading in them their standing and ability. His eyes were cold and unfeeling as those of a cottonmouth snake's and his face was devoid of expression. He was a killing machine, cold, deadly and efficient. Vance Brownlow felt his wife's finger bite into his arm as the eyes looked at her, then he knew the chill of fear as Parsons looked at him. Vance was no coward, but he was no fool either. He knew that here was a man who would kill him without batting an eye or turning a hair to do it so fast that he would never know just what happened.

"Brownlow!" said Parsons, in a voice that had all the brutal finality of the croak of a buzzard dropping to pick the eyes from a corpse. "They tell me you've hired a fast gun to take care of you. Let's see him."

"I've hired no one," Vance began. "I——"

It was then Dusty moved forward, cutting off Vance's angry denial. "Nobody hired me," he said gently. "But I'm the one you want."

Parsons inclined his head in acknowledgment. His guess at Dusty's ability, capability and identity had been correct. With this thought in mind the killer began to give out a warning to the others, although he never took his eyes from Dusty's face. The slightest split second of inattention would be enough, against a man as fast as Dusty Fog, to be fatal. In that thought Parsons did Dusty far less than justice, for the small Texan would never take an advantage of any man. However, Parsons judged all men by his own standards.

"I passed a word about Brownlow here," he said. "There's only one way you can ride for him. By passing me."

Stone Hart was the leader of the Wedge and to him it would have fallen to take up the challenge, but Dusty had taken the play from his hands. Stone knew his own speed and limitations. He was a good man with a gun, but he was way out of his class against a man like the gaunt killer. He would send down his hand with all his speed, grip the butt of his Colt, perhaps even start to lift it—but he would be dead before he could raise it higher and long before he could get it lined for use. Now it all rested on Dusty, he'd called the play.

"Three to one, Parsons," Dusty asked gently, without relaxing his watchful attention on the killer, and with good cause. "Or do we make it three to three?"

"Call it any way you want, Captain Fog."

"Mark, Lon!"

At the words Dusty's two friends moved forward, Mark stepping to the right and the Kid to the left, halting on either side of Dusty and standing relaxed but ready.

The room fell silent, only the ticking of the clock on the wall sounded. The diners at the tables, the waitresses backed towards the walls and Mother Handy by the side of the cash desk, all were silent, hardly breathing, as they watched and waited for the next move in this deadly game.

"When you're ready, Mr. Parsons," said Mark gently.

The gunman facing Mark licked his lips. There was sweat pouring down his face, for suddenly the odds in the game became too even for his liking. It was an easy thing to scare off cowhands when backed by Iowa Parsons. It was no longer an easy thing when faced with even numbers, more so when the three were men like Dusty Fog, Mark Counter and the Ysabel Kid.

"I'm out," was all the gunman said and backed towards the door. He passed through it and went along the street to the livery barn, collected his horse, picked up his thirty year gatherings from the hotel and rode from town.

The Ysabel Kid's face split in a cold grin as he moved back. He was the slowest of the trio and could most be spared in this matter. There was no fear in this decision, for the Kid did not know fear. He would have gone up against Iowa Parsons even knowing he had no chance, if such a deed was needed. Right now it was not needed, for Dusty and Mark were quite capable of handling matters without his help. Now one of the other side had yelled "calf rope", and backed out and the play was one to one.

Parsons acknowledged the Kid's departure only in that it left him in a better position. Mark Counter stood on the other side of Dusty Fog, away from the man who stayed to fight. That gave Parsons an advantage, or so he thought, for Mark would have to be firing across his friend's front.

"We're leaving, Parsons," Dusty said quietly.

Iowa Parsons started his hand lashing down. It was a fast move, one which showed practice and skill. Dusty had watched the other man's eyes, saw the flicker which gave him warning and sent his hands crossing to the bone handles of his matched Colts. The twin Colts came into his hands, lining and flame licking from the four and three-quarter-inch barrels towards Parsons. Mark was moving and a split second behind the crash of Dusty's Colts, ahead of Parsons' move, the long-barrelled ivory handled Colt lifted from leather, hammer drawing back and filling to spew lead out.

The crash of shots shattered the silence of the room. Smoke laid down its whirling eddies around Dusty and Mark, but they knew that Parsons and his man had not made it at all. Parsons had brought his gun from leather, but it was not lined when the two .45 bullets smashed into him and hurled his body backwards through the door off the sidewalk and into the dirt of Tombstone's Toughnut Street. The other gunman spun around, crashed into the wall and went down, his gun not yet clear of leather.

The room was silent again after the shots flung back their lash echo from the walls. The raw, acrid smelling powder smoke wafted back in the breeze through the door, biting into Birdie Brownlow's throat as, with a cry, she turned to her husband and buried her face into his shirt, Vance's hands went around her, but his face had lost all its colour. Stone Hart and his two men stood stiff and silent. They'd all seen Mark and Dusty in action, but that speed gave a man pause to think no matter how often he saw it.

Dusty looked back at Vance, his face and voice hard. "Go and see about getting your crew, and take your lady with you."

It was left to Stone Hart to make the first move. Stepping forward, he laid his hand on Vance's shoulder, putting life into limbs which would no longer obey the dictates of the mind. Vance Brownlow had seen Wyatt Earp showing his speed and skill on a target in preparation for the forthcoming Pistol Shoot. Never had the rancher seen the real thing until this day. Now he'd seen it. That was no paper target which stood before Dusty Fog's bone handled Colts. It had been a living, breathing man, a man filled with hate and the urge to kill, a man who had killed for a price many times. Now all that was left of the man was a crumpled pile of clothes, an empty holster, a mass of quivering flesh, slowly spreading blood in the dust and dirt of Toughnut Street.

At the door, even as the crowd started to run along the street towards Mother Handy's Eating House, Stone Hart halted and looked back at Dusty Fog.

"I'll hold three places for you, Dusty," he said quietly.

"Do that, *amigo*," replied Dusty. "And if you send any of the boys in for supplies, send them in threes. It'll be safer."

Then Stone Hart was gone, taking Vance and the sobbing Birdie with him, followed by his two hands. Dusty glanced at Mark, who was standing over the second gunman, looking down to make sure he was beyond any help. Mark's eyes lifted

nd met Dusty's, he shook his head, walked back and joined
is friends to await the coming of the Tombstone law.

It was Mother Handy with her broom who drove back the
rowd of eager onlookers who were trying to enter the room
nd see the man who shot down Iowa Parsons. The old woman
ad spent all her life in the west and in her time had seen many
f the fast men in action. She'd heard often of Dusty Fog's
peed, but as far as she could remember had never heard of
ow good Mark Counter was with his guns. Good he was, she
new that now. Iowa Parsons was the man many had said would
vin the Pistol Shoot and yet he died of a case of slow. There
vas more, the old woman could swear that Mark's guns had
leared leather ahead of Iowa Parsons' draw and that the tall
'exan could have faced him, drawn and walked away from it.
'he thought made Mother Handy frown, then she understood.
Mark Counter rode in the shadow of the Rio Hondo gun wizard
nd his own skill went unnoticed.

The crowd parted and Mother Handy removed her broom
o allow Texas John Slaughter and a stocky, rubbery looking
nan in a store suit, entrance. The man wore a gunbelt, but did
ot have the look of a real fast hand with a gun. On his lapel
vas the badge of County Sheriff; his name was John Behan.
'he old woman allowed the two men to pass her, then gave a
varning that she would break the head of the first man who
ut his foot inside the door without good cause and followed
hem to the table where Dusty, Mark and the Kid waited.

"You, Dusty?" asked Slaughter, jerking his thumb over his
houlder in the direction of the grisly thing in Toughnut Street.

"He wouldn't have it any other way."

Behan nodded gravely at the words, turned and told some
f the crowd to remove the two bodies and get them to the
ndertaker's shop near the jail. Then he turned his attention
ack to Dusty.

"Parsons was a real fast man, Captain Fog," he said. "There's
ome it won't suit to think you took him fair."

"I saw it all, John Behan," snorted the old woman. "So just
et any of that dirty Law and Order bunch try and make me
ut a liar."

At that moment Virgil Earp arrived. He came alone, with
one of his brothers or their friends to back him. That was his

way of showing good faith, for he'd been told who was involved in the killing and knew the situation needed careful handling if shooting was to be avoided. The Texans had little love for the Earps and what they stood for, Virgil knew that all too well. By coming alone he was leaving himself a way out in case some hot-headed fool wanted Dusty Fog and his friends arrested.

"What's all this, John?" he asked.

"You can read the signs, Virgil," answered Behan. "Iowa Parsons met up with a better man. That's all."

That was all, unless Earp wanted to carry it further. It was common talk around the town that Iowa Parsons had put the Indian sign on Vance Brownlow and said no man must hire to him. It was also common talk, so fast did news travel in western town, that Vance had locked horns with Rambeau, the killer's boss and had been backed in it by the three Texans. That Iowa Parsons, so proud of his reputation as a fast gun killer and bender of wills, could not overlook. He must come out and face down the men who dared go against his word. He had done so, the end was on the street being borne off on to the cold slab in the undertaker's shop on the first leg of its last long journey. There was nothing to be made of the shooting. It was justifiable homicide. Dusty Fog had defended his life even to the extent of taking life from Parsons, and in the West that was no crime.

"You was first here, John," Earp said evenly, his face showing nothing of how he felt. "I've more than enough work of my own."

The crowd who watched from outside felt disappointed at the words. They all knew how the Earps and Behan stood. They also knew that any Texan was likely to be more friendly to the sheriff than to the Earps. So they'd hoped to see Virgil Earp take a firm stand on the dignity of the Town Marshal's office. In that case there would be more action, for no Texan would willingly surrender to a Kansas lawman. Now there was no chance of it, for Earp was walking towards the door, leaving John Behan in charge. The crowd broke up, some to go about their business, the others to head for the undertaker's shop and peer through the windows at the sheet covered forms on the slabs.

Behan waved a hand towards a table and suggested they sat down. The others all complied and he looked straight at Dusty, for a moment he looked, then turned his eyes to laughter:

"Texas John, can you get Captain Fog out to your place for a few days? At least, until this blows over."

"Sure. It'd be best, Dusty. Otherwise the *Tombstone Epitaph* will be asking why Johnny didn't arrest you or run you out of town if you stay on. The *Epitaph* is backing the Law and Order bunch and it'd be a good way to get at John here."

Dusty knew this to be true. The *Tombstone Epitaph* was a violently pro-Earp paper and would make much of the fact that Sheriff Behan did not arrest the man who killed Iowa Parsons. Forgotten in the story would be the fact that City Marshal Virgil Earp, in whose jurisdiction the killing happened, did not make the arrest either. All the blame would be heaped on to Behan's head, the truth distorted and accusations of Behan being a friend of Dusty Fog thrown out, showing that the friendship was the only reason why Dusty was not arrested. The newspaper would use this incident, given a chance, to blacken still more the name of John Behan in the eyes of the voters.

"Stone Hart's taking out a herd for Vance Brownlow and running them into Tombstone," Dusty answered. "We'll ride with them and that way we'll be right clear of town until just before the County Fair."

Slaughter slapped his hand on the table in some delight and Mark grinned broadly, for he also saw what Dusty was getting at.

"The Earps and the *Epitaph* won't dare say a word if we come in with the herd," Mark drawled. "Reckon the trail drive crew'll be something special, having brought meat into town. Folks'll surely allow that Wyatt's trying to get men who might-lick him in the shooting matches out of town so they can't enter. That'd sure lose him friends and voters."

"You're right on all sides, for once, Mark," agreed Slaughter. "We'll play it that way then. Comes the day you're going to be on hand to give Earp a real shock."

So it was decided and Dusty, Mark and the Kid left the Eating House to head for the livery barn to collect their horses and head out for Stone Hart's camp. The three young men walked along the street and there was some nudging and pointing as they passed. The word of the death of Iowa Parsons had made the rounds and in the Bucket of Blood saloon the bartender was amazed at the amount of people who came in to lay bets on the small and insignificant man he'd marked down at ten to one, but who now stood at even money, and whose odds Leslie was thinking seriously of putting even lower still.

Dusty, Mark and the Kid were passing a shop window, when they came to a halt and faced the glass, staring at the display inside. The shop was opposite the jail and a shotgun armed deputy sat on a chair on the jail porch, his undivided attention on the window.

The entire window space was taken up with a sloping surface on which, in niches, were set the prizes for the two shooting matches. There were cased pairs of Remington, Smith and Wesson, Merwin and Hulbert and other kinds of revolvers along the top of the slope, for the firearms companies of the East had given freely to have their weapons on show at the Cochise County Fair. Along the sides were various rifles, also donated as prizes; these framed the first prize of the Rifle Shoot and the first and second prizes of the Pistol Shooting match.

Resting on two pegs, framed by the red baize cloth, was the prize which brought the Ysabel Kid to a dead stop and put a look in his eyes that no woman ever had. It was a Winchester Model of 1873, .44.40 in calibre, yet such a weapon as the Kid had only seen the once. The woodwork was of the finest black walnut, polished and shone to reflect the scene, checked and engraved by a master craftsman. The metal work was of finest deep blue colour, engraved in a manner which pleased the eye. The sights were the finest, closest a man could ask for and there was a set trigger capable of the finest adjustment a man might want to make. Inlaid in the butt was a silver plate on which were the words, "Presented to", a space for the winner's name, "First Prize, Rifle Shoot, Cochise County Fair". On the top of the barrel would be engraved just four words, the greatest understatement in the history of the Winchester Repeating Firearms Company: "One of a Thousand".

Yet it was nearer to one in ten thousand that so perfect a barrel was found as to warrant the added care and attention which went to make such a rifle and give it the right to bear that title. That then was the prize in the rifle shoot. It was a prize the Ysabel Kid swore in the most solemn lodge oath of the Comanche Dog Soldier that he would win and own.

Beneath the box, in a case with a special leather holster, a brass skeleton carbine stock and a set of carbine type sights set on the frame over the chamber, was one of the long barrelled Colt Peacemakers such as carried by Wyatt Earp. It was the second prize in the Pistol Shoot.

Below this, in the center of the window, in the place of honour, lay the first prize for the man with the fastest double draw of them all. The mahogany box lid was raised to show the brass plate on which was engraved:

"COCHISE COUNTY FAIR PISTOL SHOOT WINNER"

In the box, held and caressed by red felt, were a pair of matched, pearl handled, gold inlaid Colt Cavalry Peacemakers, their metal work of the finest blue citizen's finish and chased with gold in a manner that no other guns from the Colt factory ever had. They were fine guns and would make the winner proud to own them.

"Now there's what I call a fancy brace of guns, Dusty," drawled Mark. "I reckon they'll look swell on the wall in Ole Devil's study back home."

"There's only one thing to that, Mark," replied Dusty. "One of us has to win them first."

Mark laughed. "With luck I might get that long-barrelled Colt gun, but you'll be taking that fancy pair of guns with you when we leave."

The Kid could not tear his eyes from the rifle and had not heard a word his friends said. To the Kid a revolver was something just to be toted along for use when no great accuracy was called for and his knife would not answer the question. That rifle, that wonderful Winchester, was all he was interested in.

With a final glance at the window, Dusty turned and walked away. He knew that even if he won the guns they would never see use, but would be left with his Uncle. He had little use for the idea of the long-barrelled revolver, but Mark stood a good chance of winning it. Mark turned to follow his friend, then noticed the Kid was not following them. He turned back and saw the way the dark youngster stood. A grin came to Mark's face and he poked the Kid hard in the ribs with his forefinger.

"Hey, Lon," he said.

The Kid perked as if wakened from a deep sleep. He looked at his friend with unseeing eyes, then they were drawn back to the rifle again. Mark jabbed his thumb home again and the Kid swung around.

"Huh!" he growled. "What's wrong now?"

"Just a couple of Rambeau's men lining shotguns on you," Mark replied with a grin. "I never saw you look at any gal, not even Juanita Estradre, like you're looking at that Winchester there."

"You could be right at that, Mark. I'm going to have that rifle or die in the trying for it."

"Ambition's a wonderful and inspiring thing, *amigo*," drawled Mark, grinning broadly. "But give me the first choice of the remuda and I'll take me a pretty gal 'most any old time."

The Kid stepped from the window, crashing into something which gave a very feminine gasp and began to apologise. Then he saw the smiling eyes and pretty face of Cindy Alban through the mist which surrounded him. The girl staggered slightly and her escort, the young actor, Hamish, steadied her. Cindy's face held a smile but it flickered, for the Kid did not appear to recognise her. Without being vain about it, Cindy knew she was a pretty girl, not unattractive to the opposite sex. She felt rather piqued that this handsome yet so young looking boy should have forgotten her so soon. It was only that morning she'd been chatting gaily with him as he rode beside the show wagon; then he'd been polite, attentive, and now he hardly appeared to recognise her at all.

"I'm sorry, ma'am," said the Kid, then gave a start. "Why, it's you, Miss Cindy."

"It has been for the last minute or so," she replied tartly, then she realised the Kid was not even now giving her his full attention. His eyes flickering back to the shop window and that wonderful rifle inside. "Have I changed so much since this morning?"

"Yes, ma'am," answered the Kid absently.

"You'll have to excuse him, ma'am," Mark put in. "He's got a real bad attack of Comanche fever."

The girl looked anxiously at the Kid's face. It certainly did not show any sign of fever.

"Is he all right?" she gasped.

"Why sure, Miss Cindy. It's a disease that hits a Comanche when he sees a repeating rifle."

The girl glanced at the shop window and for the first time realised what was in it. She saw the way the Kid's eyes were drawn back to that magnificent rifle and her annoyance rose again. Then she started to smile as she remembered all he'd told her of his plans on the way into Tombstone.

"Well," she said with a smile, "I never ran second to a rifle before."

It was then the Kid came above water and he realised how he was acting. The grin which came to his face was boyish and infectious and the girl could not hold her annoyance any longer.

"Hi, Miss Cindy," he said. "Fancy meeting you here."

Cindy raised her eyes to the heavens. She could sense that Hamish had drawn back and took a delight in teasing him.

"Now he recognises me," she remarked. "I hope you can see me better on the stage tonight. I suppose you will be coming to the opening?"

"Waal no, ma'am. I don't reckon I will."

"Why not?" demanded Cindy. "Don't you want to see the play and hear me sing?"

"I'd sure enough admire to do both, ma'am," answered the Kid. "And likely will when I get back."

"Back?"

"Why, sure, Dusty, Mark and me have taken on to drive a herd of cattle in for a rancher. We'll be back before the Fair starts, so you can save me a seat up front."

The girl looked at the innocent face and tried to reconcile his appearance with what Madame Paula had told her of the Ysabel Kid. It was hard to believe so young an innocent a boy could be all Paula said he was. It was then Cindy remembered how the Kid came around the bush and faced the Apache to save her life.

"Say, Lon," drawled Mark. "Ole Dusty's moving on and looking back to us like he wants something."

"Reckon he does at that," replied the Kid, looking to where

Dusty stood further along the sidewalk. "I'll likely see you when I get back, Miss Cindy——If I make it."

The girl tried to read something in the face which was suddenly cold and as impassive as a Comanche Dog Soldier's. "Will it be dangerous?"

"Shucks, no. Maybe a lil bitty stampede or two. Maybe rustlers. Could be a few hundred head of Apaches after us. It won't be too dangerous."

"Said danger's going to start right now," growled Mark. "Happen you keep Dusty waiting much longer."

The girl tried to decide if the Kid had been teasing her and was not entirely sure. She managed a smile, saw the twinkle in the Kid's eyes and the smile grew broader and brighter.

"The best of luck then, Lon," she said. "I'll try and think about you once a night——for about five seconds. Take care of him, Mark."

The girl watched Mark and the Kid walk away, then she felt Hamish's hand on her sleeve and looked at him with a gay smile.

"You look awfully serious, Miles," she said. "Don't you approve of my friends?"

"They're all right," was the grudging reply.

"For talking to, but for anything serious I prefer someone in my own walk of life. Say a tall, handsome hero who can save me from all the villains."

Hamish felt his cheeks burn and knew they must have reddened in a manner he'd not known since he first became an actor. He did not know what to make of the words, for twice when she'd been in peril he'd failed to do anything spectacular. Then he felt the girl squeeze his hand.

"Yes," she said gently. "A boy like the Ysabel Kid might be all right. But a man who'd rather look at a rifle than a girl— well, there's not much future for the poor girl, is there? Now come on or we'll be late for rehearsals. And when you kiss me in the last scene," she looked up at him with sparkling eyes, "make it look as if you mean it."

Hamish started to walk along the street by the side of the girl. He was conscious of eyes turning towards him and the pretty girl by his side. That was how it should be, he was used to it. He squeezed her arm gently and felt the pressure back on his own. It did not look as if he need bother about the Ysabel Kid or any other man, now.

Dusty, Mark and the Kid rode up to the Wedge camp and received greetings from their old friends. Short, stocky Silent Churchman, who belied both names when roused; heavily moustached, miserable looking, medium sized Peaceful Gunn, who would always ride a good two inches out of his way to avoid trouble; tall, grizzled and capable Waggles Harrison, the segundo, all greeted the three riders delightedly. Doc Leroy, tall, slim, pallid and studious looking, his store coat with the right side stitched back to leave clear the ivory handle of his Colt Civilian Model Pacemaker, turned from where he was checking the supply of bandages and other gear he used for his doctoring chores, raised a hand in a cheery salute then went on with his work. The old cook, Chow Willicka, short, clean-shaven and quick, paused in his tirade against his regular louse, grunted as he saw who was here and went on with it once more. Young Rin, the wrangler, the night hawk and the four men Stone hired to supplement the crew for the drive, all looked on. They did not know who the three Texans were but they did know *what* they were.

Stone Hart sat with Vance Brownlow and his wife by the fire and looked up with a grin.

"See you made it, Dusty," the trail boss said. "I took on all the hands I need to ride the herd through. How about coming along as shotgun guard?"

"A good idea," agreed Vance. He'd been worrying about how Stone would get on if Dusty rode with them. Dusty had a reputation as being a trail boss and might not take to riding under another man. He did not know that Dusty would have been just as willing to ride as a hand and take orders as he would to take command. Dusty had been a soldier and knew that to lead men one had to be ready to take orders as well as give them.

"We'll ride with you like that," Dusty agreed. "When do we pull out?"

"Right now. I want to put a few miles between us and Tombstone," Stone replied. "There's a chance Rambeau might try and scatter the remuda, or shoot up the camp and I don't want to take a chance on any of the crew catching lead."

So it was arranged without fuss or bother. Dusty was to ride with Mark as a guard while the Kid went ahead as scout. The herd must be brought through and they aimed to see it was.

CHAPTER SEVEN

A Chance Offered

Vance Brownlow rode between Dusty Fog and Stone Hart towards his old white-walled Spanish style house. The building was in the grand style of the old *hacienda* made by men who had plenty of good, cheap labour and wanted a home which would last for centuries. The house stood in the center of large grounds and was surrounded by a high parapeted wall from the safety of which riflemen could pour lead down on any attackers. There was but one entrance to the grounds, through a large, steel-studded, heavy wooden gate which looked strong enough to stand up to an artillery pounding. All in all the place looked as if it was built to be used as a fort—and had been more than once.

It only took one look at the building down below to tell Dusty that Vance was no man's fool and that he could stay alive in this wild country as long as he had plenty of supplies, water from the well in the ground and ammunition. In the grounds of the house was a long line of stables in which the personal mounts of the cowhands were held, while the main remuda was out in the corrals, under the wall, where they could be covered with rifle fire if need be.

Looking around, Dusty tried to catch some sight of the herd, but could not do so, which surprised him. The country rolled up into the foothills about half a mile away, but all around there was little or no cover and certainly nowhere near enough for a herd of five hundred head to hide in. The herd must be held somewhere near the house or the Apaches would have jumped it before now.

"We made it safely," Vance remarked. "I thought they might try to hit us at the crossing of the Carne River."

"Lon said there was Apache sign up there, but it was old," Dusty replied. "I reckon that'll be where they aim to hit the herd. We'll all be too busy handling the cattle to keep a good watch."

"We've got to get the herd moving fast," Stone pointed out, looking around him, clearly puzzled as Dusty had been, at the lack of sign of the herd.

"When do you mean to start out?" asked Vance as they rode through the gates, which had been opened by his foreman and a cowhand.

"At dawn comes the morning," Stone replied. "Make a fast run and hope that we aren't being watched."

The Ysabel Kid and Johnny Raybold drew their horses to one side and allowed the others to ride on by them. For three days since leaving Tombstone they'd been on the scout and what they'd found confirmed that the Apaches were about, just waiting for a chance to hit the herd.

Hooking his leg up over his saddlehorn, Johnny looked around with some considerable care. "We're being watched, Lon," he stated.

"Sure," was the laconic reply.

"Scouts for the Apache?"

"Likely."

Johnny extracted a sack of tobacco, took out papers and rolled two smokes, his fingers working as if they had eyes of their own. He passed one cigarette to the Kid, who rasped a match on his thumb and held it towards the tip of Johnny's weed. The smokes were going and the two men sat their horses drawing in the tobacco fumes and exhaling them once more.

"Never rode scout against Apaches," Johnny remarked, not for the first time. "Hoss-Indians, like your kinfolk, are more my line."

"Man'd say they're the worst of all the tribes," answered the Kid. "Grandpappy Long Walker always used to tell me he claimed one Apache coup counted for two against any other tribe."

Johnny thought over the words and they gave him little comfort. It was not bad praise, coming from a war leader of the Dog Soldier Lodge, a branch of the Comanche Nation noted for being great fighting men in their own right.

"Where'd the scouts be?" Johnny asked, as he finished his smoke and carefully put out the stub before throwing it away.

"Out there somewhere," drawled the Kid, waving a hand to the open land before them.

The smoking had not been the sole reason for Johnny and the Kid staying out here after the others had gone in. All the time they'd been smoking their eyes had been flickering around, checking every inch of the ground ahead of them for some sight of the Apache scouts their instinct warned were watching.

Johnny had been born and raised in Indian country and had learned the tricks of the Indian scout early and from necessity. He knew the ways of Indians—but as he said, they'd been Comanches, Southern Cheyenne, Kiowa, horse-Indians all. The tribes Johnny knew did their moving, scouting and fighting from the back of the "god-dog", that wonderful four-legged creature which came to them from the early Spanish Conquistadores. Johnny knew the ways of such Indians and knew little or nothing about Apaches. The horse-Indian scorned excessive stealth as a way of war and any fighting he did was from the back of a racing war pony, plainly, openly and with spectacular results. The Apaches were different. They used the horse, but not to the extent of the plains tribes. True, given a war relay, an Apache would run a grain fed cavalry troop into the ground, but the Apache would do that same thing on his own two feet given a start across his type of country. The Apache was just as at home on his two feet as he was on a horse and he would fight from cover, in ambush if he could, preferring to take life in war, rather than lose his own through lack of caution.

"I don't see them any place," Johnny remarked after another moment's hard searching of the ground ahead.

"You wasn't expecting them to stand on top of the rocks and wave signal blankets, now was you?"

"Was they Comanches, I might. Comanches don't have no better sense," scoffed Johnny, then became more serious. "You got any of them spotted, Lon?"

"Think maybe I spotted one, about half a mile away out there. By them two rocks that are side by side. I could be calling it wrong though."

Johnny reached down to his saddlepouch, where he carried a pair of powerful field glasses for just such an emergency. Before he could take out the glasses he was stopped by the Kid shooting out a hand to grip his wrist.

"No go, *amigo*," warned the Kid. "They can see us and likely know what those glasses are for. Happen they reckon we've got one of them spotted they pull out and hide up again, only this time we won't get to see them. Let's ride on in and tell Stone what we've seen."

"We haven't seen anything," Johnny pointed out.

"Sure, that'll please him. Show him we're doing our work."

The other men were already in the grounds and dismounting when the Kid and Johnny rode towards the gates. Already Vance's foreman was showing the men where to leave their horses. Stone looked around, saw that his men were being attended to and got down to serious business.

"Let's ride out and see the herd, shall we?" he asked.

Vance nodded. "Sure. I'll take you while Birdie and the cooks throw a meal together for the hands. Are you coming, Dusty?"

"Sure, you've got me puzzled, where you're holding the cattle."

The Kid and Johnny rode up at that moment, dismounted and walked up to the trail boss. In something that might have been called a military brace and with his hand raised in a mocking salute the Kid asked, "You ready to hear a report of the activities of your scouts, Colonel, sir?"

"Sure, make it fast, we want to ride out to the herd," Stone answered.

"They're watching us."

Stone waited for a moment, but the Kid remained silent, so he grunted. "That's a tolerable fair report."

"Tells us about what we already know," Dusty went on. "They're not going to try and hit the herd where they'll be up against men with rifles, men who know the ground. That's not the Apache way. They know the herd's been gathered for shipping and they're just waiting and watching until they know which way you're headed before they hit."

"They'll pick their time and place, when they know which direction we're headed," agreed Stone. "How many scouts are there, and where?"

"Now you've hit a point, Stone," replied the Kid with a grin. "Two at least, three at most. I reckon I'd got one spotted for sure and could make a fair guess where the other two are."

"There might only be the one, if that was all you saw," Vance objected.

"Sure, there might, but I didn't see him for sure. Just finding one's as likely as drawing a queen into the middle of a four card straight flush," the Kid replied. "Apaches aren't fools, Vance. Don't you sell them short on either brains or military knowledge; that's where the blue bellies make their mistake and it costs them lives."

"You'd better explain to us then, professor," Vance replied, but he was listening attentively for all the light-hearted way in which he spoke.

"Sure, one lone man gets bored. Gets to thinking about his squaw, or some pretty lil gal who threw a stick at him, which same means to get herself all set up to be courted kind and loving. Two or three of them on scout, they watch each other as well as what they're scouting for and make sure there's no sneaking away done. Likely they meet up somewhere each night and stay together, no Apache likes being alone in the dark. That's why I conclude there's at least two and at most three of them watching you out there."

"But this is fairly open country. Where would they hide?"

"Not too close in, Vance. They could see you moving the

herd from a fair piece back. But don't go betting they're not in close. An Apache can hide where you might reckon a jackrabbit'd show up real plain."

"Could you find them, Lon?" asked Dusty. "And get rid of them?"

"Likely, given two or three days, Johnny and Peaceful to help me and a whole lot of good luck. If we went out and started looking now, they'd just pull back and we couldn't chase them far enough away to let you get the herd moving without their knowing it."

"The Apaches would be suspicious if you tried it," Stone remarked. "We'll pull out at dawn and play them as they fall."

"Which same's the only chance we have right now," Dusty agreed. "Let's leave this hard-worked scout to get a meal and head out to the herd."

The three men took their horses once more and rode out through the gates. Vance took the lead and looked around him with some curiosity. He'd covered most of the ground ahead of him hunting or bird shooting at various times and thought he knew it well. Now he was beginning to wonder if he did know it so well after all, if three Apaches could be hiding so close, watching every move made at the ranch.

Then Dusty saw a narrow gorge in one of the hills, an opening with a pole fence across it. Two men sat by the fence, smoking, each with a rifle across his knees and a belt full of bullets slung over his shoulders. They raised their hand in greeting, dropped from the rail and advanced to meet the three riders.

"The herd's in there," Vance remarked, indicating the opening.

On drawing closer, Dusty could see that the opening might be narrow but beyond it a wide valley was exposed to view, a valley where a fair-sized herd of cattle were grazing. A nearer approach showed that the slopes of the valley were very steep and in places had been made steeper by human hands. The area was a large blind canyon and being used as a natural and very useful corral. The cattle in the canyons were all well fed and looked healthy enough.

"There's a spring and a small stream in there. It goes underground at the blind end," Vance explained a point which puzzled Dusty before the small Texan could ask about it. "I can hold up to five hundred head in here for a fortnight or so. More if I hay them down to help out the feed."

"That's not a bad idea," Dusty answered.

"I found this canyon while hunting for wild turkeys," Vance replied. "Saw how it could be put to use, steepened the sides where cattle might be able to get out and tried it. It works all right. How about the herd, Stone?"

"They look fit and well enough," Stone replied. "I'll not go in and disturb them. You've got a fair head of white faces among them."

"It's part of a herd I brought in with me. I hope to change the cattle all to whitefaces soon, they make better beef and cause less trouble than longhorns."

"Sure, but will they live off the country like longhorns do?" Dusty asked.

The technical discussion lasted until they had stabled their horses and were entering the house. Vance insisted they were his guests and would stay in the front where he and his wife lived instead of bunking with the hands in the now over-crowded bunkhouse section. The invitation was also extended to Mark and the Kid, for Stone wanted to hear their view on the conditions the drive would be made under.

With the meal over, their gunbelts and hats hanging on the pegs by the front door, the men went out to sit on the porch. Birdie, dressed now in a gingham frock, came out with a tray containing coffee pot and cups. She poured out coffee and handed the cups around, then sat on the arm of her husband's chair and looked towards the men who were risking their lives to bring the herd in.

"How do you figure to get the herd to Tombstone?" she asked. "And don't tell me walking, that I know."

"The way we came out here. Swing up to that ford and miss the wooded country. That way we'll be in clear land all the way. We could lose half the herd if we got into the woods, even if there was a ford and we don't know of one."

"Reckon Lon could scout the woods, just in case?" Dusty asked. "We know the Apache are thinking they'll grab the herd and the river's their best spot."

"That's for you to handle," Stone replied. "You're chief of

scouts on this drive. I don't like the idea of going through those woods unless we're hide-bound forced to do it."

"I don't like that gap we have to run the herd down about a day's drive from Tombstone," Mark put in. "I thought as we came through it'd be a good place for an ambush."

"Not from Apaches that close in," objected the Kid. "I reckon if we can get the herd across the Carne River we're clear of Apaches. They'll not come too close to Tombstone."

"I wasn't thinking about Apaches," Mark answered. "Rambeau's not going to give up that easy. No Syndicate man ever does."

"That's what's puzzling me," Dusty remarked. "I've heard some about the Syndicate and this sort of thing isn't in their line at all. They run saloons, gambling houses, places like that. They don't bother with cattle rustling, for that is what Rambeau's play comes down to. Why'd they risk getting involved in something that could blow up in their faces and cause real trouble?"

"The money on the herd will be a tidy sum," Vance replied.

"About half of their take for the day across the country," Dusty answered. "I reckon the Syndicate doesn't know what Rambeau's doing. That he and Parsons were planning a private deal. We'll have to hope that Rambeau keeps quiet about it. The Syndicate wouldn't want it known one of their top guns was planning to pull a deal on the side with a saloon operator."

"Then it might be as well if they found out," Vance remarked.

"That depends on how much word has got around. The Syndicate run because of their reputation for being tough. How's it going to look to the folks who they keep down by fear if word gets out that somebody has bucked a Syndicate man's play and shoved his face into the mud?"

The others did not speak for a moment. Then Stone said, "They'll make Rambeau back his play on his own and either come through or go under."

"He could have hired some more guns by now," Mark pointed out. "The Syndicate won't send him any more of their top-grade stock and he'll be on his own, sink or drown. That's why I reckon he'll hit at us in that draw. It's his first and last chance. He won't want to risk it too far away from town and then likely wind up with Apaches riding over him. Nearer, folks might hear, then come to see what all the shooting's about."

Vance Brownlow looked at the other men. They were all so calm and cool, not one of them showing the slightest apprehension at the thought of fighting their way by a horde of Apaches only to find more fighting against the guns of a power-greedy man. He felt confident that his herd would get through now. He also saw that had he been left to make the drive alone, he might have been wiped out without even knowing where he'd gone wrong.

"Do you think we could pull out now, make a fast run for it and be gone before the scouts know what it's all about?" he asked.

"We could try, but I wouldn't want to. The scouts aren't alone, there's a decent sized bunch somewhere, maybe two, maybe five miles away, maybe even more," grunted the Kid. "The scouts would hear the herd being moved and they'd light out. They don't like fighting in the dark, but they'll move by it. They'd get to the bunch who're near at hand, then we'd have them hit us at dawn, when the hands are all getting tired and slowed down. They'd do enough damage, run off the remuda, wreck the chuckwagon and be gone. And they'd go right to the main crowd to let them know we're on our way."

The other Texans nodded their agreement. They'd all a fair knowledge of tactics and knew the Kid called his shots right true to the center of the target. The surprise moving of the herd would not remain a surprise for long and the pursuit would come faster than any herd of cattle, much less a herd of white-faces, could be pushed.

Mark opened his mouth to make some suggestion, then closed it again as he came to his feet along with the others. They all heard the distant crash of shots and Vance Brownlow's face lost much of its colour as he looked at the others.

"The herd!" he gasped.

"Too far off for that," replied the Kid. "There's a fair bunch of riders coming this way."

It was some moments before any of the others could even

hear the sound of rapidly approaching riders. By that time the Kid could make out certain sounds which gave a clue as to who it was approached.

"I'll get the hands," Vance said.

"Don't get all into a mucksweat," replied the Kid. "Shod hosses, leather creaking and metal clinking. Them's white men coming. An Apache couldn't make so much noise even if he wanted."

"We'll just get our guns afore we open the gate though," Dusty answered.

Guns in hand, Vance carrying a magnificent double-barrelled shotgun, the men sprinted towards the gate but, despite the Kid's warning, Dusty opened the barred slot, keeping well to one side and called, "Shout up, who are you?"

"Open the gate!" came the answering shout, "Cavalry here!"

Dusty threw open the gate just wide enough for one man to enter at a time. "Come ahead slow and easy," he ordered. "And come with your hands empty."

The first man to enter was a grizzled and tough looking cavalry sergeant, riding with one hand on the reins, the other held waist high and well clear of his gun. He did not look alarmed or surprised at the caution shown by the occupants of the house.

"Take it kind if you'd hurry, gents," he said. "We just had a run in with a small bunch of Apaches and one of our men's carrying lead."

Mark caught Dusty's nod and opened the gates to allow a double file of blue clad, campaign hatted cavalry men to ride by him, followed by a young officer who holstered his long barrelled Colt as he came through the gate.

Sliding down from his horse, the young man looked towards the group of armed cowhands, then towards Birdie, who was coming with a lamp, then to the armed men who came pouring from the house, carrying lights with them. His face was pale and it showed signs of having been involved in the first fight. For all that he was in full control of himself as he saluted Birdie politely.

"Good evening, ma'am, gentlemen," he said. "We've just had a brush with the Apaches. One of my men caught a bullet, so when we saw your lights I came down here."

Birdie turned to where a young trooper was leaning forward in his saddle, a wound in his shoulder running blood down the blue tunic.

"Get the boy off his horse," she snapped. "Doc! Doc Leroy! Come and look at this soldier."

Doc came fast and the trooper was helped down from his saddle, to be taken up to the house. The young officer told his men to take care of their horses, then stood looking back through the look-out slot of the gate.

"How many of them did you get, mister?"

The lieutenant turned quickly, for he knew that sort of voice. It was something a green young shavetail fresh out of West Point could tell well enough, the tone of a tough officer addressing a junior. His eyes went to the small Texan who stood ahead of the others. There was something in the way Dusty stood that warned the officer his guess was not wrong. Here was a man used to asking questions and getting quick and accurate answers.

"I believe we dropped three."

Dusty swung around and snapped, "Mark, get Lon's old Blackie hoss, Lon, happen the lieutenant here'll let you. I want you to go out with the sergeant and take a look around where they hit the Apaches."

"I'll do just that," answered the Kid and headed to the house for his gunbelt, going at a dead run.

The young officer stood beside Dusty and looked with open admiration at the huge white stallion Mark led up. "I wish it was time of war," he said. "The Army's allowed to make compulsory commandeerings of remounts then, you know."

"I'd heard something about it," Dusty answered dryly. "Mister, there aren't enough men in your whole regiment to commandeer that horse from the Kid."

Once more the tone was there. The voice of a senior officer addressing a West Point plebe who gave unasked for information. There was more to this small man in cowhand dress than first appeared. It was with a considerable effort the officer managed to avoid stiffening to brace and making a formal apology.

The sergeant touched his hat and requested permission to ride with the Kid and the young officer gave it. The gate was opened and the two men rode out into the night.

"Could I night here, please?" asked the officer when Vance introduced himself. "I'm on a long sweep out of Fort Grant, checking on Apache movement. There's been a lot and I have to swing back up to Black Falls, then make my way back to the Fort."

"Stay here if you like," Vance replied. "I'm afraid we're a bit crowded at the bunkhouse, but they'll make out."

Dusty remained by the gate when the others went back to the house. He'd been standing there for a few moments when dark, then Stone asked:

"You thinking the same way I am, Dusty?"

"Why, sure. The time's only eight o'clock now. We could work up a tolerable head start if things fall right."

They heard the sound of hooves and, although neither spoke, both knew the other was tense and eager to hear what the Kid had to say when he returned. The horses drew nearer and Stone opened one side of the heavy gate, then closed it behind the Kid and the sergeant.

"Three of them," growled the Kid, sliding from his saddleless white.

"We rode into them by accident," the sergeant went on. "Young Darcy's all right. It's his first time out on independent command, but he never lost his head. Got the men through, was the last to leave himself."

"Did you hear any Apaches getting away?" asked Dusty.

The sergeant was a thirty year man, he knew a born leader when he saw one and knew that small, or tall as a redwood tree, here was a leader born, bred, raised and fully ready to lead.

"Were just the three of them as far as I know," he answered.

"Call it that way myself, Dusty," agreed the Kid. "Was I asked, that is."

"Take it you're asked."

"Three of them, small camp, likely no more," drawled the Kid. "Man'd near be safe betting it's the scouts."

Stone and Dusty's eyes met and there was the same thought in both their heads. However, the ultimate decision rested on Stone as the trail boss. He made it fast, without asking Dusty to share in the final responsibility if things went wrong. That was the way of a man like Stone Hart, or of a man like Dusty Fog. It was the way of a leader of men, of a trail boss.

"Roust out the crew, Dusty," he said. "I'll tell Vance and his lady to be ready. We ride in one hour."

Dusty turned and went without another word. Time was valuable now. The three scouts were dead and the herd could be got started without word reaching the waiting Apaches until late the following day. The actual time would depend on when the scouts were due to be changed or to report to their leader.

In the big dining-room of the bunkhouse section Dusty found a crowd of men, Vance's regular crew, the Wedge cowhands and the soldiers. There was much good natured chaff among the men and Dusty stood at the door for a moment. The talk died down and he raised his voice.

"You Wedge hands all comfortable after your long ride?"

"We sure are, Dusty," whooped young Rin.

"I aims to go to bed and sleep until the drive starts," one of the new hands went on.

"Which same's in lessn' one hour from now."

"Good, then I'll—WHAT!" The answer began cheerfully enough but ended in a wild yell as the full import of the words hit the man.

"One hour at the most," Dusty answered. "Get them moving, Waggles. Stone wants the herd headed up and moving before nine o'clock."

The segundo did not need twice telling. He'd made this sort of fast move before and was on his feet giving orders without even having to think twice about what he was saying or doing.

"Rusty, Silent, go with young Rin and help the night hawk with the remuda. Peaceful, you'll take point with me. The rest of you know where I want you. Grab your gear and hit the front of the house—*pronto!*"

It was lucky that the men had not unloaded their bedrolls from the wagon. Vance had offered the loan of blankets for the night to save them unpacking and time would be saved. So there was little to do in the orderly rush as the men prepared to pull out.

Birdie, dressed in her jeans and shirtwaist, still tucking the flap in the back of her waistband, came into the room, paying no attention to the choice and highly coloured language which was flying around. She found Chow Willicka, who was throwing his borrowed apron off, leaving Vance's cook to deal with the feeding of the newly arrived soldiers.

"I bet your wagon's nowhere's nearly ready to roll," she jeered.

Chow sniffed loftily and chose to ignore the words. He and Birdie got on very well, although they were in a state of feud all the time, which kept them amused and which the hands found highly stimulating. The old man turned to a young soldier who sat near at hand.

"Huh!" he grunted. "Women. Don't you never go and trust one, son."

The sergeant was standing close at hand and gave his agreement. "Had me a gal back at home. One night I told her that if she didn't marry me I'd up and join the Army."

"And what happened?" asked Birdie.

"She said yes, I married her—and joined the Army a month later."

"Which same only goes to prove what I allus said——" began Chow.

"Go boil your fool old head!" Birdie snapped, then she and the cook were headed for the door to harness the team of the chuckwagon.

Out in the grounds before the house, the scene lit by lamps brought from the house, men were mounting their horses. The two wagons were ready with teams harnessed and ready to roll. Chow gave his louse a gentle warning that he'd best stick up real close when they pulled out, then swung on to the box of his wagon. Birdie, carrying a wolfskin coat, climbed up beside him. She meant to ride the herd later, but knew she would be more use here out of the way during the tricky night drive ahead.

"Best put that coat on, ma'am," Chow said. "The night air get's a mite cold late on."

"Chow, honey," she replied with a grin as she struggled into the heavy and warm coat, "I didn't know you cared."

He grinned at her, "I don't but if you come down with a

chill you'll likely blame it on my cooking. I knows you women."

The young woman's blistering reply almost seared the paint off the wagon seat, if there'd been any paint on it. Chow chuckled, then took up the reins and started the chuckwagon forward. The gates were open and the men riding through, into the night, making for the herd.

CHAPTER EIGHT

Dust Has Its Uses

The men came towards the blind canyon, riding at an easy trot and saving their horses for the work which would come later. The two guards had heard the noise and rightly guessed what was happening. They'd worked fast and the fence was down by the time the trail crew arrived.

Stone Hart moved back and let the men through into the canyon. This was going to be a ticklish business and one that the slightest slip could ruin. The cattle had to be eased off their bed ground and got moving without being scared and sent off in a wild stampede. Stone wanted the herd moving fast, but not at stampede speed. With lesser men he might have been worried about starting the herd, but each man here was an expert, even the new hands had worked on the big interstate drives from Texas and knew what to do.

The riders entered the valley without fuss or undue noise, keeping to the edges until they reached the blind end. Then they started forward, riding slowly and stirring up the sleeping cattle as they went. Steer after steer came to its feet and began to move before the riders, not panicking, not running, just moving ahead. On the two flanks of the line of men Waggles Harrison and Peaceful Gunn gauged their time right and started to move along the flanks of the herd, the other riders following, tightening the herd of cattle, cutting the bunch down into a thin line. There was a big steer forcing his way through the herd, and as he came out of the canyon opening he found a rider on either side of him. Peaceful and Waggles had the lead steer now, they were at the point with him and would stay there with him until they reached the shipping pens. The rest of the heard followed out of the opening, the swing riders coming in about a third of the way along, then the flank men joining two-thirds of the way from the point. The last steers came out and the drag riders followed them. Back in the canyon Mark Counter and Vance Brownlow were making a careful sweep to make sure that none of the herd had been left behind. Mark was riding with the herd this night, then he would be free of all duties so as to be able to ride with Dusty and the Kid as part of the free-ranging fighting force.

The herd came out, Waggles and Peaceful steering the big leader towards the east and Tombstone City. Then as the cattle moved away Rin and the night hawk came in with the remuda, holding the horses behind the herd at a distance. Chow sat on the wagon box with Birdie beside him. He started his team forward and the wagon lurched into line behind the remuda, the bed-wagon, with the hands' bedrolls, spare gear and some equipment brought up the rear.

To Vance, riding from the canyon towards Dusty and Stone, it was nothing short of a miracle the way his herd had been got moving in so little time. Stone's hour was hardly over yet and the cattle were on the move, under control and headed for the market.

Dusty was lounging in his saddle and thinking fast. He was not bothered about the cattle, although he could admire the skilled way in which the Wedge hands got the herd up and moving. He was thinking about the three dead Apache scouts and trying to decide how their death could be turned to further advantage.

"Vance," he said as the rancher rode up. "Call back at the house. Tell your foreman to keep his guards on the canyon as if the herd was still there. Have the fence erected." Before he could say more Dusty was interrupted by the arrival of the Ysabel Kid and Johnny Raybold, reporting for their orders as scouts. This was Dusty's department, although usually it would have fallen on the trail boss to tell them what he wanted doing. "Johnny, get ahead and make a scout. Don't go too far in front, though. Lon, I want you to take a couple of Vance's hands out to those dead Apaches. Hide them and try to cover up all their sign. I know you won't be able to do it perfect, but make sure they can't be found too easy."

"I get the idea," Vance said. "You want to try and fool the Apaches into thinking the herd's still in the canyon. Then they won't follow us."

"It won't fool them long," Dusty answered. "But I always allow that any time saved is worth while."

Stone nodded in agreement to this. He was not interested in the way Dusty handled the defence or planned the strategy of the herd. Stone had been a Confederate cavalry officer too, but he knew Dusty was his master when it came to out and out planning of a campaign. Dusty was in charge of tactics, that had been the agreement they made in Tombstone and Stone was willing to let it ride that way. It was a pleasant change to have no other duties than those of handling the cattle.

Dusty and Vance headed back to the house with the Kid, and there Vance gave the necessary orders to his foreman. Turning, Vance and Dusty rode through the gates and headed after the herd. Vance was far happier now than he'd been for weeks. This was his chance, the money the herd brought in would enable him to start on the improvements he planned for his ranch.

Vance Brownlow was a man with vision and forethought. He knew that it was a matter of time, months maybe, two years at most, before the pressure of the U.S. Army brought the Apache nation to peace. Then a man could start and build up his herds, put whiteface cattle which gave good beef on to the range to grow fat on the prime grazing. The half-wild longhorns were a hardy race of cattle, but they left much to be desired in the way of beef and Vance was sure he could improve the stock. The money this herd brought in would go far to doing that for Vance. That was the prize Vance stuck for. The herd would make his dream or see it ground, into the dirt for nothing. It all depended on the skill of Stone Hart as a trail boss, the loyalty of those hard riding and reckless cowhands and their chances of slipping through the Apache net.

Stone Hart was sitting his big grulla horse to one side of the herd and waiting for them to catch up. His teeth flashed white against the dark blob of his face in the night.

"Nice so far," he said.

"Easy," agreed Dusty, stopping his seventeen-hand paint and looking ahead to where a cursing cowhand was chasing a steer back into the moving line. "We'll make us good time tonight."

That was only to be expected. The herd were range bred stock and not used to being penned down in one place for long, even in a place as well watered and offering such good and safe grazing as the blind canyon. Once they were out of the canyon mouth they were willing to head off at a good clip. They would stay bunched for safety, with the exception of the odd attempt to break off and hunt pastures new. Right now the steers were wanting to put as many miles as they could between themselves and the canyon, which had been their prison for so long, and the trail crew were in full agreement with this desire. Every mile they could put between themselves and the ranch before dawn gave them just that much time and distance ahead of the Apaches.

The wagons rolled by and Birdie raised her hand in a cheerful wave to which the three men replied. Stone smiled:

"Your lady'll be real tired come morning."

"Right now she's like me," Vance replied. "Too happy and excited to feel tired at all."

The three men started their horses again and Stone asked: "Where's Mark?"

"Riding the swing," Dusty answered. "He thought he'd give a hand until dawn."

Soon after the Ysabel Kid came up, his big white stallion moving like a ghost through the night.

"Got it settled," he said. "Vance's foreman'll attend to things. He's been around in Apache country."

"Cut off ahead then, Lon," Dusty answered. "Make a big circle and see what you can find. If you see Johnny, watch him—he might shoot you in the leg."

"He couldn't hit me unless he got the gun resting on my levis," scoffed the Kid, turning his horse. "Don't let 'em sneak the herd away from you."

The Kid's horse faded once more into the night and Stone turned his horse to head for the point. Vance rode alongside Dusty, having decided to cut himself in on the fighting side instead of riding herd.

"How does a boy as young as the Kid come to know so much about Apaches?"

Dusty grinned towards Vance. "Reckon his grandpappy might have taught him."

"Was his grandfather an Indian scout?"

"Well no, I don't reckon Indian scout quite covers it. See, the Kid's grandpappy is Chief Long Walker of the Comanches."

The herd was kept moving on through the darkness. The hands took turns to make for the remuda and change their mounts, selecting an animal from their own string even in the blackness of the night. Dusty, Mark and the Kid had spare horses borrowed from Stone's remuda and they would be able to rest their own mounts, although the three stallions would follow the herd and not be mixed with the other horses.

The time was four o'clock when Stone joined Dusty and Vance again.

"No sign of the Kid yet," he said.

"He'll likely be along when he's good and ready," Dusty replied. "You know him of old, Stone."

It was at that moment the Kid and Johnny rode up. Stone grinned. "Talked of the devil and up pops the Ysabel Kid."

"You'll be hurting my feelings soon," warned the Kid.

"Not your better feelings, you never had any," growled Stone. "Did you find anything, or have you just come back because you felt lonely?"

"I don't feel lonely," replied the Kid. "Didn't out there anyways, not with a camp of about thirty or more Apaches laying out in the brush."

Vance tried to keep up the same laconic posture and expressionless mien of the other two, but could not restrain an ejaculated "Apache camp?"

"Which same's just what I said, Colonel," drawled the Kid.

"Comes dawn they'll all be awake and on the lookout. They'll see the dust kicked up by the herd and know something's gone wrong. Then they'll trail us and hit us when we least expect it."

"We've got to stop that," Dusty said quietly, showing neither excitement nor worry. "We don't want them hanging on our flanks."

"Could you take some of the men and pin them down while the rest of us push the herd on?" asked Vance.

"Not a whoop and whistle in hell's chance, *amigo*," Dusty replied. "They'd soon know just how few men were against them, leave ten or so braves to hold us down and the rest come after the herd. You couldn't run the cattle in flat stampede far enough and fast enough to get clear."

"If it wasn't for all the dust we might run around them out of sight and hearing of the camp," Stone put in. "A camp that size will make things real awkward for us, Dusty."

Dusty did not reply, he was looking to where ahead of them the herd was moving and at the dark pall of dust which hung in the air. Then he turned his attention back to the Kid and asked:

"I don't reckon they knew you were about, Lon?"

"I'm back, aren't I?"

That figured to a man who knew Apaches and Dusty Fog knew them. The Kid would not have blundered blindly into the Apache camp, and walked out again. He must have found it with the aid of his big white stallion, then reconnoitered on foot and in complete silence.

"About thirty you say?" Dusty went on.

"And all braves, not a single, solitary squaw to keep them company."

Again that figured. The Apache brave did not take his woman along when he put on the paint, took up the war hatchet and went forth to do battle with the hated white-eye brother. With women there the camp might have been just a bunch headed to a fresh camp ground. Without them it only meant one thing. War, fight for the herd of spotted buffalo the white-eye ride-plenties were taking to market.

"What we really need is either a troop or so of cavalry for protection, or more men," Vance remarked, cutting in on

Dusty's racing thoughts. "And quite frankly, I can't see us getting either."

"You've got a fair idea," Dusty agreed. "A troop of cavalry is just what we need. Or at least a whole big bunch of men."

Stone was silent and watching Dusty's face, trying to pierce the darkness and read what was on his mind. He'd seen Dusty in action before and knew that already the small Texan had a plan worked out.

"Stone," Dusty said and, although Vance could not tell any difference in the tone, Stone knew things were going to move fast, "I want Mark, Silent, Peaceful, Rusty if you can spare him, and Johnny. You too, Vance if you'll get your rifle out of the saddleboot."

"It'll leave us short-handed, but we'll make out," Stone replied. "Reckon Birdie'll lend a hand with the herd, Vance?"

"Try and stop her, old boy," Vance chuckled. "I'll ride on and tell her."

"Hold hard there, Vance," Dusty cut in. "Don't go off until you know what I want doing. Tell Chow I want some empty sacks, then stop the bedwagon and cut eight lengths of rope from that coil in the back. Make them long enough so they'll hang down from the saddlehorn and reach the ground with some trailing. Tell Chow I'm real sorry, but that Stone'll pay him double time, seeing as it's after midnight."

The men scattered and in a short time Birdie was afork a cowpony riding the flank of the herd, while on the other side Rin, fetched up from the remuda, proudly rode as a cowhand. The men Dusty called for lined up before him, peering through the darkness towards the man they knew as the finest light cavalry commander the Civil War had produced. There was a tense and expectant air about them all, for they knew that something was afoot. Half the crew were here, almost all of Stone's loyal and hard riding hands. Taken with Mark Counter, Dusty Fog and the Ysabel Kid, and not forgetting Vance Brownlow, it was a fighting force to be reckoned with.

"What's on your tricky lil ole mind now, Dusty," asked the Kid.

"Real army strategy, *amigo*," Dusty replied. "And when Vance gets back I'll explain it to you."

From ahead they could hear the blistering, hide-searing curses which came from Chow Willicka as he lent Vance a hand in the back of the bed wagon. There were many highly original curses heaped on the head of Dusty Fog, for Chow did not wish to fall behind the herd, not when he might have to tire his horses catching up. For all the curses, Chow would no more have thought about arguing or disobeying Dusty's command than he would of not following Stone's word.

"Now, gentlemen," Dusty drawled as Vance rode up carrying the sacks and lengths of rope.

"Something tells me I ain't going to like this," Silent Churchman whispered to the Kid.

"Out ahead of us there's a camp of about thirty head, all bucks and all armed unless Mr. Loncey Dalton Ysabel's called the play wrong," Dusty went on, ignoring the interruption. "So we're going to outnumber them."

"Never figured you'd forget how to count, Dusty," Rusty Willis put in and waved a hand along the line. "There ain't nowhere's near thirty of us."

"That could bring a ticklish point," admitted Dusty. "Especially if the Apache get to know how few of us there really are. We've got to make sure they don't—until it's too late. That bunch has to be stopped following us and maybe picking us off one at a time from behind rocks. We've got to try and slow them down some so that they can't get to the mainbunch in time to warn them we're out. Or at least slow them so they'll not give the main bunch a chance to pick their place and hit us."

"That's fair enough, Dusty," Mark drawled. "How're we going to do it?"

"We're coming in at them just before dawn, with the wind behind us, and we're coming in whooping and yelling like a drunk Comanche coming to make talk. I want all the noise you've got, shooting, hollering, that's why I've got Silent along. Pass out the ropes and sacks, Vance."

"Chow would only part with five sacks," Vance replied.

"The rest will have to haul mesquite scrub or anything heavy behind them to stir up the dust. Pass the sacks around and then get them weighted down with rocks!"

The men all got Dusty's idea. It was a good one and, given any amount of good Texas luck, it would work. If it didn't—

well, there wouldn't be too much time to worry over it. If it failed, the only thing they could do would be try and take as many of the Apache with them before they went under.

The Apache camp was silent, the first streaks of dawn's light coming in the east. Not a brave stirred as they lay around the small fires, blanket wrapped and still, their weapons sharing the blankets with them. Every brave lay there, some dreaming of the fighting and the coups they would take, others were dreaming of the loot from the ride-plenties who were with the herd of white man's buffalo. It would be hard-won loot, for no ride-plenty ever was taken without a fight. The cattle meant little to the Apache except as a means of trade. Below the border, where the soldier-coats could not follow, were men who would trade repeating rifles, blankets, whisky or tequila for the spotted buffalo the cowboys drove.

There were no guards around the camp; the Apache was too light a sleeper to need any. Each brave slept in peace, for there was no word from the scouts that the herd of cattle had been driven from the blind canyon where it had lain safe under the rifles of the ranch crew. It was not a luxurious camp, with no wickiups set up, for there were no women along to perform this menial but essential task. The braves wore paint, they were ready for war and in war women had no place.

Of all the Apache band, only the two young boys brought along to tend to the herd watching were not in their blankets. They sat their wiry ponies, asleep on the job of watching the war relays of the warriors. The two bangtail scrub ponies of the herd-boys were also sleeping, standing, and the rest of the bunch of horses was settled down, giving no trouble and making no noise.

The wiry paint pony ridden by one of the herd boys suddenly came awake, its head jerked up and it snorted loudly. The boy astride it woke, jerking erect and staring around him, his mouth opening to let out a wolf-howl of warning. He was a full twenty seconds too late. The horses of the warriors were coming to their feet in a wild and snorting panic, eyes rolling and ready to bolt.

Deadened by the soft sandy soil, the hooves of horses sounded. A large cloud of dust welled up and from it came a hideous cacophony of wild cowhand yells, whoops, screams and the blood-chilling scalp howl of a Comanche Dog Soldier.

The young horse herder went backwards from his pony's blanket, a hole between his eyes, his startled yell ending unborn by a fast taken shot from one of the riders of the dust.

The second horse herder was lucky. His pony gave a wild leap which sent him flying from its back. He lit down with a catlike agility but was an instant too late, for the entire bunch of horses were up and running. The boy turned, hurdled a small bush, landed rolling into the shelter of a rock, where he lay out of sight until the raiders went by.

"Get the horses through the camp!" Dusty Fog's voice peeled out even above the rest of the noise.

The chief of the small band was fast asleep and dreaming of the great killing of white-eyes he would make when he traded his part of the herd for a repeating rifle. Yet from fast asleep and pleasant dreams to full awake, blankets thrown off and on his feet holding a single-shot Springfield carbine looted from a dead cavalryman in some long-forgotten frontier fight, was work of a second. The rest of the band were also waking, coming up to their feet with wild yells, grabbing their weapons. But like the herd boy they woke full twenty seconds too late.

Into the camp area came the charging, stampeding horses, the dust they kicked up more than doubling that stirred by the hooves of the attacking party's horses and the weighted sacks or mesquite scrub each man dragged.

Yelling, shooting, almost half-blind by the dust, the men charged their stampede in among the Apaches. It was one of the few times the Apaches were taken by surprise. They did not know for sure how many men were attacking them, and before their startled, sleep-slowed minds worked the horses were gone, the cloud of dust settling on the camp and billowing high over the cowhands who kept the stampede going, making sure the horses were not easily found again.

It was over and done with now. Two miles from the camp Dusty allowed his men to remove the sacks, empty them and cast off the mesquite scrubs. He wanted to be sure they were out of sight of the Apaches before allowing the dust to settle. The camp had been disrupted, the braves scattered and running in all directions, disappearing behind rocks and under bushes in the Apache way. It would never do to let them see how small a force was involved in the raid. The Apaches might run before a sudden and unexpected attack, but they'd be ready and willing to take on the cowhands if they found out how few the party numbered. They would hit all the harder and with more savage rage to recover their lost face.

The Apache horses scattered, sped on their way by shots and wild cowhand yells. Not one of those half-wild broomtails would stop running until it was exhausted and that would not be for miles. The Apaches would have a long time ahead of them before they caught their scattered mounts. It would take them time to get to the main bunch on foot, too, Dusty was sure of that.

Bringing his big paint to a halt, Dusty waited until the dust settled, then turned to the others, a grin splitting his face, which was covered in dust.

"Coil up those ropes and empty the sacks," he ordered. "And take the sacks with you. We might need to pull that game again."

Through the mask of dust and grime the Kid grinned, his white teeth a strange contrast. "It's not likely to work twice. Fact being I didn't even reckon it would work once."

"We were lucky," Dusty answered.

"Lucky nothing, Dusty," snorted Vance. "You planned to hit them while they were asleep, take them when they least expected it. Now they don't know for sure if the herd's moving or how big an escort we have."

"Could be your guess's a meat-in-the-pot hit," chuckled Mark. "Only don't let ole Dusty know it. He'll take on airs and then half a dozen or so of us'll have to settle on him and talk him back to normal. Last time he took on airs that way was when he read what some Yankee colonel said about how he handled Troop C of the Texas Light in the war. It took eight of us and a couple of hours to tucker him out and throw him in the hoss trough."

Vance laughed, then he turned to look at Dusty with fresh interest. "Of course," he said. "You're *the* Captain Fog. I never connected you with him. You couldn't have been very old then."

"I was seventeen," Dusty replied. "Almost eighteen when the war ended."

"Gad! I heard about you. Colonel Houghton-Rand, my old commanding officer, was out here as a military observer with the Union Army. He met you when you killed that General in a duel."

Dusty smiled, lounging back in his saddle. That was long ago, but he still remembered the day when he faced General Buller on the field of honour and killed the Union Army officer. The British colonel had been his second and Dusty remembered him well. That Vance had heard of Dusty was not surprising, for in the War Dusty's use of his troop had changed military thinking on light cavalry tactics.

There was no time now to think back about the old days, to dream of what might have been had the South won the War. No doubt Dusty would now have been at least a colonel handling a regiment. However, he was not worried, he was content with his lot and the men he led. The OD Connected ranch's crew were as good as any regiment.

"Let's get back to the herd," he ordered as his raiding party finished emptying the sacks, casting off the mesquite bushes and coiling the ropes.

Vance rode by Dusty Fog, silent for a time, then he laughed.

"Something amusing you, *amigo?*" Dusty asked.

"I've been cursing this dust ever since I came out here," Vance replied. "But now I'm going to change my mind. Yes sir, Dusty. Now I know that dust has its uses."

CHAPTER NINE

The Kid Brings Word

"Come and get it afore I throw it to the hawgs!"

Chow Willicka rubbed his hands on his apron and let out the time honoured bellow which served the cowhand as did mess call the soldier. The old cook stood by the big stewpot, ladle ready to fill the plates of the hungry trail crew as they filed past him.

It was the fifth day out from the ranch, the herd was making good time and there'd been no sign of Apaches since busting up that bunch on the first morning. For all that, Dusty did not relax his vigilance. He, Mark and Johnny rode a circle around the moving cattle, the Kid ranging far ahead. Then two days back the Kid had come to the chuckwagon as Chow and Birdie served out the morning meal. He asked for and was given dry rations for three days, then rode out. That was the last they'd seen of him, where he'd gone and what he was doing was known only to Dusty Fog and Stone Hart.

Dusty collected his food and joined Stone by the fire. Not even the trail boss was allowed to take his meal off the lowered

103

boards at the rear of the chuck-wagon, that was the cook's private domain. So Dusty and Stone settled down on their haunches, as they'd both done so many times before.

"No sign of the Kid yet?" Stone asked.

"Not likely to be tonight," Dusty replied. "The river's still two days away. He's not riding a relay."

Stone nodded thoughtfully. The Kid was scouting the ford of the Carne River for possible Apache ambush. It would take him time and he would have to rest his big white stallion after so much hard and gruelling work. On the Kid's news depended an important decision. The Carne River was for most of its length fast and with high sheer walls dropping down to it. There was only one way to get the herd across that Stone knew of. To the north lay a place where the banks shelved down in a gentle slope and the river widened to make a deep, slow moving pool through which the cattle would swim with little or no difficulty. It was a two-day drive, about twenty-four miles to this ford, although the river itself was only about one day's drive from them in a straight line. There was a small snag to that. Stone did not know in what manner the river stood straight ahead, for this side's banks were thickly overgrown with trees and bushes. To try and push a herd blindly into thick wooded country like that would be asking for trouble and could result in the loss of a good half of the cattle.

The woods had been a source of much discussion between Dusty and Stone. It didn't take a master-mind to figure the Apaches would have the main ford under heavy guard, if not actually covering it in full strength. But there was no sense in pushing blindly into the woods if they were to find the river impassable through the same high banks which marked most of its length. It would be foolish and worse than foolish to drive the cattle into the woods, then find they had to turn upstream and use the main ford anyway. That was one of the reasons the Kid was riding scout now. To see what the ford in the open country looked like and then try and find a second way they might cross the river.

Dusty finished his meal. It was dark now and other men were starting their usual horseplay, engaged in what had become a favourite pastime, stirring up a feud between Birdie and Chow.

"Say, Miz Birdie," Rusty Willis called. "I sure bet you made this stew."

Birdie grinned. "I did, how did you know?"

"Easy. Old Chow's tastes like he's washed his shirt in it," Rusty answered. "Now yours, why ma'am, it tastes the same, 'cepting you use that fancy smelling ladies' soap."

"How long have this bunch been like this?" Birdie demanded, eyeing Chow belligerently.

"They was all right until they started eating women's fixings," Chow answered. "Which same goes to prove——"

"It doesn't prove nothing, 'cept that they've had their tastes spoiled by a wored out old chow wrecker," Birdie yelled back.

The argument grew more heated by the minute, yet for all that there was nothing in it. Chow found having Birdie working with him a most novel and stimulating experience. On the ride out to the ranch she'd left him to handle things and he'd been polite, well spoken, on his dignity around her. Their relationship was strained for the first day, with Chow bottling up his feelings and admonishing his regular louse in so gentle a manner that the gangling youngster thought he was ill. Then on the second morning he'd heard Birdie cursing one of the team horses in a manner which left nothing to be desired to breadth of knowledge or depth of fluency. From that moment on Chow carried on as normal and his louse breathed a sigh of relief.

Dusty and Stone listened to the argument growing, laughing at the retorts which flashed back and forwards. Then, with their meal finished, they went to the bin of hot water and dropped the plates in. Coffee mugs in hand, the two men headed for the bed wagon. The back was let down and a lantern hung inside it. Birdie used the wagon for sleeping and her bed roll was spread ready. Stone climbed into the wagon, went to where a small box was firmly fitted to the side. He lifted the lid and took out a large Army map of the area which he'd brought from Vance's ranch. Moving back to the end of the wagon, he sat on the board and spread the map out. Dusty leaned by the wagon and in the light of the lamp they started to study the map once more, checking over the details of the range with their memory of the trip out.

"Still worrying over that map?" Vance asked as he walked towards them.

"Sure," Dusty agreed. "Have you ever run a herd into Tombstone before?"

"No, this's the first shipping herd I've been able to move since I took over. The man I bought the ranch from ran two in."

"Which way did he go?" Stone inquired.

"Up to the ford where we crossed, but the Apaches were at peace then. He told me he'd seen a small hunting party as he was crossing the river."

Stone ran a finger along the map, following the course of the Carne River. He tapped a cross marked on the river's coarse.

"There's another crossing here."

"I know," Dusty agreed. "Six days' drive over rough country. We'd never make Tombstone in time for the Fair and a herd this size wouldn't bring much of a price there at any other time."

"We'll have to decide by noon tomorrow at the latest," Stone warned. "That's when we'll have to start swinging north to the open country ford, or south where we might be safe, even if we don't get the herd in on time."

"I'm in your hands, Stone," Vance replied, then showed the sort of spirit which made the English gentleman what he was. "If it'll save lives, I say hang the Fair and the money, take the southern route."

Stone and Dusty looked at Vance with open admiration. The Englishman's hopes were based on this herd, on the money selling it at the Fair would bring in. Yet to prevent them losing men he was willing to sacrifice it all, take the long route to Tombstone and miss the big money which the herd would undoubtedly command in the meat-starved town.

Stone grinned. "Thanks for saying that, Vance. There's few enough who would have. You took me and my boys on to get your herd to Tombstone in time for the Fair and that's what we aim to do. The Wedge has never failed to push a herd on to market and this isn't going to be the first time. How do you feel, Dusty?"

"I'm in this root, hog or die," Dusty drawled. "And I'm sure not fixing in to let any Apaches push me any place."

"Then I——"

Vance began to say something to show his gratitude, but

the words ended before they'd really begun. Dusty and Stone came off the wagon, their hands bringing the guns from leather as they peered into the darkness.

"Douse that light, Vance!" Dusty snapped. "We've got visitors."

It was then Vance heard the sound of horses approaching. He vaulted into the wagon and put out the lantern, plunging the area around the wagon into darkness. From out in the light a voice he recognised called:

"You're about two minutes too late with that, Vance. I could have dropped all three of you had I wanted."

The Kid, unshaven, dirty, his black clothes smothered in mud, the shirt sleeve torn open, rode up. He was not riding his big white stallion but sat a wiry Apache pony with two more following on a lead rope. The huge white horse came after them, without a saddle and looking as if it had done some travelling. The Kid himself had the appearance of a man who'd ridden far and done plenty.

"Rusty, Doc!" Stone snapped as the talk around the fire died down, the trail crew staring at the apparition by Stone's side. "Get over here and take care of the Kid's horses."

The two men in question rose, but Mark also came to his feet. Rusty and Doc were good hands with horses and could handle the three Apache broomtails, but the Kid's huge white stallion was another proposition. The old Blackie horse would allow only the Kid to handle it with any impunity. Even to the other members of the floating outfit Blackie showed no friendship and merely tolerated them. For any man, other than the select few, to try and handle the big white was dangerous in the extreme.

Birdie grabbed a mug from the table, filled it with hot coffee and darted forward to hand it to the Kid. He took the mug and drank, conscious that every eye was on him and that every one of the crowd was seething with questions.

"You made good time, Lon," Dusty remarked as the Kid finished the coffee.

"Man'd say you're right," answered the Kid. "I met up with an Apache headed for war and discussed him out of his relay. Made me a fast ride up towards the ford."

"How is it?" Vance asked.

"Bad, there's a good two hundred braves waiting on the ford and likely more of them about if needed."

"Two hundred?" Stone put in.

"Waal, I didn't stop to make no herd count, Stone. Just took me a quick peek, then headed out again. I've seen me two hundred Injuns afore now and know about how many it is. There's that many there, at least."

Stone did not doubt the accuracy of the Kid's words. There probably was not an exact two hundred braves there, but Stone was willing to take bets that the Kid called it to within twenty one way or the other. That many Apache would be a rough and hard handful for a full battalion of cavalry. They hopelessly outnumbered the trail crew. He asked no questions as to how the Kid came to be riding an Apache warrior's war relay. Somewhere out there the Kid must have come on a lone scout or a brave headed for the fight. What happened after that was anybody's guess. The Kid probably had not risked using his firearms for fear the noise would attract other Apaches. That meant there came a sudden, silent rush, the flash of sun off the blade of a James Black bowie knife and an Apache went to the happy hunting grounds.

"We'll have to pull down to the south ford and forget the Fair," Vance put it. "I don't want to risk losing lives."

It was not just a speech made to raise his prestige in the eyes of man. All the trail crew knew the store Vance set on getting the herd to Tombstone and they also knew he was sincere in what he said.

"There's another way."

All eyes went to the Kid as he spoke. Dusty knew that Indian dark and grim-looking young man as well, if not better, than any of the others and asked:

"What're you getting at, Lon?"

"There's a crossing on the Carne River—downstream—in the woods."

"Can we use it?" Vance asked.

"Sure we can. The banks are easy, the water's not even as fast as up at the other ford. It's fairly open country on the other side. We can use it all right—if we can get rid of five young Apache bucks who're watching it night and day."

"Like that, huh?" Dusty drawled.

"Just like that," agreed the Kid.

The others all fell silent, Birdie and Chow were no longer bickering and the rest of the hands sat waiting to hear what their fate was to be.

"Five of them couldn't hold the ford against us," Vance remarked, putting his thoughts into words.

"Nor even mean to try," replied the Kid. "See, Vance, they're not aiming to hold us up, or even fight us, not on their own. That'd be a foolish play and whatever else they might be, Apaches aren't fools. They'll be waiting on the river there, watching all day, for the first sight of the herd. They know the country, know how a herd'd have to travel to have grazing and water. They know that come noon tomorrow if you're in sight of the woods that's where you'll be going, not up to the open ford to the north."

"They might have more men in the woods then," Vance remarked.

"Not unless they moved in since I left."

Something in the way the Kid spoke warned Vance, told him a story. He looked at the unshaven, gaunt and tired face and knew that the Kid must have personally searched the woods, moving in complete silence to find the Apache scouts.

"Tell it, Lon," Dusty said gently.

Sinking to his haunches the Kid went on, "I came downstream after scouting the other ford. Found the tracks of five hosses and followed them. The hosses were staked out with a couple of young 'uns guarding them. I was afoot and went quiet. The other three were resting just inside the woods, but watching all the same. I let things lie, didn't figure I could take five of them and any noise'd send the others heading off fast. I didn't figure you'd want them either killing or scaring just yet awhile, Dusty."

"That's good figuring," Dusty answered. "It's no good warning the Apaches up at the other ford that we know about this one. I reckon their chief's just covering all the bets by having this ford watched. He doesn't expect us to use it."

"You called it right. The scouts are boys, look like they've just been took in on the lodge and are being given this chore as a test. They likely have been told to run as soon as they see the herd, if it comes their way."

"What would happen then?" Vance inquired. "You said the main bunch was at the other ford, right up to the north."

"They are, but they could get down here and on to us before we could get over the river and far enough towards Tombstone, so it wouldn't be safe for them to follow us further."

Birdie came forward, halting to stand before the men, hands on hips and glaring at them.

"That's enough for now," she snapped. "Lon, I've got a plate of stew for you, it's over on the wagon boards. Go and eat it."

The Kid looked up at Birdie. He knew she was born and raised in the cattle country, she knew that only by the cook's permission could the right to eat at the wagon board be given. Then he saw Chow giving a nod of agreement and realised he was being granted the supreme honour of the trail drive, he was being allowed to dine on the cook's sacred territory.

"Dusty may not have finished with the Kid, dear," Vance put in.

"He has," she snorted, eyeing Dusty and daring him to object. "That poor boy looks as if he's not eaten since he rode out two days ago and I'm not seeing all you well fed yahoos standing around asking him questions until he's good and fed."

Vance smiled, then said, "One thing I learned early during my marriage was never to argue with Birdie. You always wind up in second place."

The Kid rose and followed Birdie to the chuck wagon and was soon eating a good meal. The men around the fire all sat back now. They'd done their day's work and most of them would be taking a turn at the night herd soon.

"How about it, Dusty?" Stone asked, for this matter came under the province of the fighting leader rather than the trail boss.

"It's the woods, down to the south or an early grave," Dusty answered. "And given the choice, I'd take the woods to the river. The crew would only have to try and hold them in something like a bunch. We might lose a few head but we'll get the rest over, what's more we'll make Tombstone alive, instead of some Apache's wickiup as a war trophy."

Stone chuckled. He might have felt annoyed at Dusty suggesting a way to get the cattle through the woods, but he did not. Dusty had put into words the thoughts Stone himself had on the problem of the woods and the solution. Now it all depended on whether Dusty's fighting scout force could get rid of the Apache scouts and make sure any more who came were also dealt with.

"When that poor, tired lil boy's had his food, took a bath and rested a mite, we'll ride," Dusty said. "He can use one of the remuda horses. I'll take Mark, Johnny and Lon with me. You'll have to let Peaceful ride close in scout."

"Could I come along?" Vance asked.

Dusty looked at the rancher and grinned. "You're getting to be a regular ole glory hunter, Vance."

"Was his hair shoulder long I'd call him Custer," agreed Stone, also grinning.

"Dash it all, there's nothing in that," Vance answered. "I merely want to go along and see how you handle things. I've done a considerable amount of hunting and hope I won't get in the way."

"You come along then," Dusty answered. "What sort of things have you hunted?"

"Bear, mountain lion, bighorn sheep out here, stag in Scotland, boar in the Westphalia of Germany," Vance replied.

"Man who's done that much hunting shouldn't need us to help him then," drawled Dusty. "Say I met a rancher up on the edge of the Indian Nations. He come from England. He told me about hunting wild pigs with a spear and from a horse, did you ever try that?"

"You mean pig-sticking," Vance replied, grinning. "Only once, while I was on leave at Canton, in China. At least the chappie swore they were wild pigs. It turned out later we'd skewered some rich chappie's prize breeding hog. He was annoyed."

It was gone midnight when Dusty led Mark, the Kid, Vance and Johnny Raybold from the camp. The Kid had eaten well, been to the waterhole near the camp site and scrubbed himself free of the dirt and dust, changed into a fresh black outfit from his warbag and caught up with a brief sleep. For all the fact that he'd been sleeping lightly and uncertainly for the past couple of nights the Kid looked fresh and alert as if he'd been safely in his bed at the OD Connected each night.

Vance and the Kid drew ahead of the others. It was a rare tribute to the rancher that the Kid allowed him to ride up front on what amounted to a scout, as much a tribute and honor as was the Kid's allowed to feed off the chuck wagon boards.

The two men rode along in silence, but after a time they brought their horses to a halt. A sudden noise and crashing through the night ahead of them again brought movement. Vance's hand shot down as he leaned forward to jerk the Winchester rifle from his saddleboot. The Kid swung across and caught the rancher's shoulder.

"Don't bother, it's only an old scrub bull taking off," he drawled.

The sound of the animal's rapid departure faded into the distance as Vance straightened once more. He peered through the darkness towards the Kid.

"How could you be sure it wasn't a man?"

"Ole Blackie here told me."

"But he didn't do anything," Vance objected.

"That's how I know. If it'd been a man ole Blackie'd have pointed him like a deep south bird dog aiming at a bobwhite quail."

"The Apache might have men out there though," Vance went on.

"Might, but it's not likely. All their men are gathered up there at the open ford, except for the scouts. The braves have gathered. I reckon I must have got one of the last on his way. Just stop your hoss a minute and listen."

The horses halted and Vance strained his ears, listening, trying to catch some light sound which might tell him what the Kid could hear. There was nothing but the ever present yipping of coyotes, the more distant bellow as an old scrub bull let out a challenge to the world in general and other bulls in particular. In the distance another bull answered. Off in the other direction, faint yet still with the menace it always held, came the scream of a cougar. These were the only sounds Vance could hear, these and the ever chirping noises of the night insects.

"I can't hear anything but the usual night noises," he finally said.

"Or me," admitted the Kid, "and as long as they're there I'm happy. Man comes along and those same noises stop. I bet that Johnny knows just where we are, from back there a piece by the way the coyotes have stopped yipping our way. Listen, see if you can tell where Johnny's bringing Dusty and Mark along from."

For a moment Vance did as he was told. The coyotes appeared to be calling all around, then he realised that the sounds were not coming from behind. A few seconds after he made out the faint noises of horses' hooves.

"Listen real good and you'll hear the leather creaking," the Kid went on.

Vance strained his ears but the riders were in view, dark blobs against the blackness of the range, before he could catch the faint sound of leather creaking. The Kid's Indian keen ears had picked up the same faint sound at a far greater distance. Vance could see now why back at his ranch Dusty showed such complete faith when the Kid said it was soldiers who approached through the night.

The three horses loomed up out of the night and Johnny asked somewhat tactlessly, "All quiet, Lon?"

"Nope," sarcasm dripped heavily from the Kid's soft spoken reply. "We're fighting Apaches off on both sides."

"Let's go," Dusty answered before Johnny could think up a suitable answer. "I want to be on those Apaches before they know we're about. That means getting to the woods before dawn."

The men rode on and once more Vance was amazed at the way the Kid acted. This was a new range for him and yet without the slightest hesitation he was taking them where they wanted to go. Vance knew that with compass and map he might be able to aim for a given point and reach it, but the Kid used neither. He relied on the inborn instinct granted to him by the blood of his Comanche forefathers. It was the ability of a travelling Indian to find his way from one point to another without any aids other than his sense of direction. This time the Kid had traversed most of the journey in daylight, coming from his scout of the river to the herd. For all of that it was no mean feat for him to find his way back to the river through the night.

Soon after the others catching up, Dusty and the Kid held a quiet conversation, then the Kid faded away, his big white stallion moving in the silence of a wild thing. The Kid had refused the loan of a remuda horse to use on the scout. He had used the captured Apache relay for his work and the white was still fresh enough to handle this raid. The Kid had complete faith in the huge white stallion he called Blackie, the horse had been specially trained for such things and was able to locate hidden men, then give the Kid a warning of their presence. Also the white would stand, not fastened, like a statue for as long as the Kid wanted and would never make a sound to betray it or its master.

Time passed, the other men rode in a straight line, not talking now, for they were approaching the river and Apache ears were very keen. It was surprising how far the sound of a voice carried at night. Vance had seen some action against Chinese bandits while in the British Army and knew that as well as did the Texans.

Vance's ears were working at full power but he still received a shock when the Kid's white horse stepped from behind a bush. He heard the Kid's gentle chuckle and knew the others were almost as surprised as he was.

"They're in there someplace, Dusty," whispered the Kid. "Ain't camping the same place as last night. Never thought they would be. They won't sleep the same place two nights running if they can help it."

"What do you reckon?"

"There's a hollow ahead, got water, good graze. We could leave the hosses down there, then move in on foot and find the camp."

"Lead on to it, *amigo*."

The men left their horses standing in the hollow and gathered. Dusty told them what the Kid found out. He looked them all over and then made his decision.

"Johnny, stay here, keep the hosses out of sight and quiet. Vance, you'll come with us. Take rifles along."

Johnny did not argue at this moment. He knew Dusty well and knew that this was not the time for argument. He was better able to handle Dusty and Mark's big stallions than was a comparative stranger like Vance. Those two horses did not take kindly to strangers being around them, or trying to handle them and it would take a horseman of the first water to control them.

Vance drew the rifle from his saddleboot, slowly worked the lever to put a bullet into the camber, doing it so as to make as little noise as possible. He was just a little worried, for the slightest slip might mean the Apaches would be scared off, running to warn the others. If that happened, the main bunch would come down to attack the herd.

CHAPTER TEN

In the Woods

"This's far enough!"

The words, no louder than a whisper, came from Dusty Fog as he sank to one knee under a tree. Behind him Mark Counter, the Ysabel Kid and Vance Brownlow also sank down. They'd made their way to the edge of the woods and moved in only a few yards when Dusty came to a halt.

"What is it, Dusty?" Vance whispered.

"No sense in busting around here and making noise in the dark. We'll just settle down and wait until it's light enough to see."

The four men settled down as Dusty said, resting their backs against three trunks. Vance was more tired than he could remember, for he'd been on night herd the previous night and spent the day in the saddle. His head was nodding and the Kid whispered in his ear:

"They're not too far off. I can hear their hosses moving."

"Are we moving in on them, then?"

"You find them and I'll move in," breathed the Kid in reply.

"They're not by the hosses, that's one thing you can bet on. Try and get some sleep. One thing though—happen you're going to snore—don't."

Vance rested his head on the hard, upstanding root of the tree against which he leaned. He shook his head slightly, trying to clear it. To the best of his knowledge he did not snore and doubted if he would even go to sleep with such a hard pillow.

A hand clamped down on Vance's mouth, while another shook him. He tried to struggle but the grip was too strong. His eyes opened and he found that it was now almost fully daylight. Mark held on to Vance until sure that the rancher was fully awake and would not make any sound, then released him. Vance sat up, carefully working his stiff and sore limbs, he looked around. Dusty was leaning against a tree, keeping out of sight behind the trunk. Of the Kid was no sign at all for a moment, then he was back. Coming through the bushes with the silence of a ghost, his rifle in his hands.

"You full awake yet?" Mark asked gently.

"Awake and ready," Vance replied, working his fingers to get the stiffness out of them.

"Found them, Lon?" Dusty asked, although he knew the answer.

The Kid's answer was grimly eloquent. He jerked his head towards the bushes and gave a gentle warning. "Go quieter than quiet, all of you."

The others rose and exchanged looks. This was the moment. Right now could be the beginning of safety or the end of the herd and most probably the lives of every man and the woman who rode with the cattle.

The men fanned out, they used every bit of cover they could find, flitting from bush to bush like shadows, avoiding treading on any branch which might snap underfoot and give warning. Vance showed the others their faith in him was fully justified and he thanked his stars that he'd always loved the outdoors and hunting. As a boy he'd poached rabbits and pheasant on neighbouring estates, done it in a day when a keeper would not think twice before firing on a poacher with a shotgun. Right now the training was standing him in good stead. It was a dangerous game he was playing and there was much at stake.

The breeze, light, shifting constantly in direction as it surged through the trees, came to Vance and his nostrils caught an aroma. It was there for a moment, then gone again, but he could have sworn he smelled the rich and appetising fumes of cooking turkey.

The Kid was ahead of the others, moving with the silence of a black dressed ghost. Then he halted, seeming to freeze in midstride. He looked back to the others, held up his hand, then moved his arms, spreading them out in a signal. The other three men advanced, fanning out. Vance was on the outside of the group, with Dusty next to him. The rancher reached a bush, peered over it and stiffened.

They were just ahead, four dark, squat, half naked young braves around a small fire. Even as Vance watched he saw one of the braves carve a slab of meat from the breast of a cooked turkey which was impaled on a stick placed in the ground. There was a small hole dug in the ground in the very embers of the fire. Vance noticed this, even more than he noticed that all the young braves had knives at their belts and their weapons were stacked nearby.

Slowly the Kid raised his rifle and the others also started to lift their weapons ready to shoot. There was no time to think of the rights or wrongs of shooting down the braves without a chance. These were Apaches, tough young braves who were on the warpath. At such a time no Apache would think twice of shooting down a white man from ambush and without warning.

There was a slight movement which caught the corner of Vance's eye, a splash of colour where no such colour should be. His senses were alert and he started to turn, dropping into a crouch as he did so. That movement saved his life. There was a hiss and he felt a burning knife-like agony well through him as the feathered shaft on an Apache war arrow drove into his shoulder. He saw the young Apache standing in the bushes, his own rifle fell from his hands. With pain welling through him Vance stood dazed, unable to force himself to make a move as the Apache fetched a second arrow from his quiver, set it and started to draw the bow string. Time seemed to be standing still for Vance and later he would never remember the incident in terms of seconds, which was how it happened.

Dusty heard the slight sound and turned, his short Winchester carbine coming up and spitting even as the brave was pulling back his bowstring. Dusty moved and shot fast, Vance later was to swear he felt the wind of the bullet on his face. The Apache spun around, his arrow jerked from the string and clattered to the ground, then he followed it.

There was no time to waste on the shot Apache, or even on caring for Vance's wound. Not right now, for the four braves by the fire were on their feet, startled and not sure where the attack was coming from. The confusion was only momentary, the turkey went into the fire, knocked over by a brave who leapt for his rifle. Three of the Apaches were moving, hurling for their weapons, the fourth turned to run.

Mark Counter's rifle crashed and one of the braves reeled, went to his knees then crashed down. The Kid's old yellow boy spat out, hunching over and dropping a second warrior even as his reflexes started to propel him towards his weapons. The third young brave was fast, he dived forward with hands reaching down and missed a fast thrown bullet from Dusty's carbine by inches. Lighting down rolling, the brave brought off a fast taken shot which ripped a hole through the brim of Mark's costly white Stetson hat. The penalty for missing came fast, thrown through the .44 barrel of the Kid's old rifle, slammed home on the end of a flatnosed Tyler Henry bullet.

The last brave was older, more battle wise. He also knew his orders in case of a surprise attack by the scouts of the ride-plenties, the cowhands. Not for him to stand and fight. Leave that to the young braves, the name-making braves with no coups to show for victory or tales to sing around the camp fire. The old warrior had done both things and needed no boosting to his name and fame so he could leave the young men to fight and die while he headed upstream as fast as his war relay could run, make his best time to warn the main band that the herd of white man's spotted buffalo would come through the woods and cross the Carne River here.

On his knees, wincing with pain, Vance tried to withdraw the arrow. He'd seen the sudden, wild and explosive burst of action and saw the brave running for the trees even as the others went down before Texas rifles.

"Quit that fooling, Vance," Dusty warned as he saw what was happening. "Set back and watch the Kid."

Vance released the arrow and Dusty helped him to his feet, allowing him to see what was going on and take his mind from the agony he was in. Vance, even though his shoulder throbbed and hurt, could not help but admire the cool way the Kid handled his rifle.

The Apache was gone, diving into the bushes like a greased weasel. He appeared for a brief instant and Mark's rifle kicked bark from the tree behind, while he went from sight once more. The Kid did not fire. He held his old rifle to his shoulder, left eye closed, right sighting carefully along the scuffed old barrel. The Kid knew that rifle, knew every vagary of it and he knew that he would have just one good chance to down the Apache.

There was a red flicker between two trees, the flicker made by the trade shirt of the Apache as he darted between two bushes on his racing way to where the horses were staked out. Vance sat it, then saw the Kid alter his aim slightly. Once more that red flash showed and the Kid's rifle barked. The red shirt jerked, staggered, crashed down. There was a thrashing in the bushes and then all was still once more.

Bounding forward with the speed and grace of a buck Apache, the Kid went into the clearing. He hurled the bodies of the three young braves, seeing in passing there was no danger from them. He also found time to cast a disappointed glance at the charred remains of the turkey on the fire. There was nothing the Kid liked more than Indian-baked turkey. Right now he had other things to worry about. He knew he'd sunk lead into the fleeing Apache but must make sure the brave was dead. He'd seen a badly wounded Apache cover ten miles once, to get where he wanted to go. If the brave was not dead he might even now get away and succeed in his duty of warning the main bunch.

Moving fast the Kid came to where the Apache lay. There was a hole in the side of his shirt, it was small, at the other side the exit hole of the bullet was large and ragged. There was no danger, the twenty-eight grain load used in the old Winchester 66 rifle might not have long range hitting power, but up to fifty yards would stop a man, especially when it smashed through the chest and burst the heart in passing.

The Kid did not stop by the Apache, he went on, ears straining to catch any sound which might warn him that there had been one or more braves with the horses and that they were now running. No such sound greeted him and he came on the Apache ponies hobbled and grazing in a small valley. The Kid made a quick circle of the valley, then after making sure no Apache had left, he turned to head back to the camp. There were five war relays and three horses each down in the valley, they would make a useful addition to Vance Brownlow's remuda.

"We'd best look to that arrow, Vance," Dusty remarked as soon as the Kid went from sight.

Vance was still gripping the arrow shaft, trying to pull at it, although he felt as if the strength was drained from him. He was on his knees and the sweat rolled freely down his face. Mark came forward, rested his rifle against the trunk of a tree and grunted:

"You stop that, Vance," he said, then to Dusty. "The danged fool's trying to pull himself inside out."

"You always did reckon a man who settled in Arizona didn't have good sense," Dusty answered. "Best tend to him or we'll have Birdie after us for not taking good care of him."

Taking a knife from his pocket Mark stepped forward and cut the rancher's shirt away from the wound. He worked fast and Vance stayed on his knees, making no sound of protest. The arrow's tip just showed from under his collar-bone and Mark only needed the one look to tell him all he needed to know.

"That's a barbed war arrow, Vance," he warned. "It won't come out the way it went in so——" Mark spoke gently, put his left hand against Vance's shoulder to hold it firm, gripped the arrow shaft with his right and forced it forward so the barbed head was clear.

Vance's body gave a convulsive heave but that was the only sign of pain he gave, except that the sweat was pouring down his face. Through his clenched lips he managed to grit out:

"Don't worry none about it. It's only me."

"Which same's why I'm not worrying," Mark answered cheerfully, cutting the barbed head off. "It's all over and done with now, isn't it Dusty?"

Then before Vance realised what was going to happen it was all over and done with. Mark gripped the wounded shoulder

again, took hold of the headless arrow by the flighted end,
gave a quick pull and it slid back through the hole and out.
This time Vance did give a yell, the world appeared to be
roaring around him. He clutched weakly at Mark's leg as blood
began to flow.

"Whisky—flask in my pants pocket——" he gasped.

Mark nodded, he felt for and extracted the small hipflask
from Vance's pocket then removed the cork and poured the
raw liquor into the hole. Vance's entire body writhed and jerked
in agony as the whisky bit into the wound. He groaned but did
not cry out, although his eyes were suddenly filled with water.
By the time he'd recovered and cleared his eyes Vance found
Mark was ripping his shirt to make a bandage. The Kid was
back from his scout, grinning broadly as he examined the ar-
row-head.

"Wonder if this here arrow's all poisoned?" he asked, knowing full well the Apache never poisoned his arrow-heads. "Had
me an uncle one time, back home to Texas. He took him a
poisoned arrow in his shoulder, swelled up like a fattening
shoat. My drinking uncle, Si, mistook him for a shoat and
butchered him for dinner. There wasn't half a to-do when they
found out the mistake. See, Uncle Ezra, him that got butchered,
he'd stashed away a whole jug of corn likker and none of the
others knew where it was."

"You damned black heller," growled Vance, with a blanket
curse which took in the whole Ysabel family. "Can't you think
of anything more cheerful to talk about than that?"

The Kid grinned and went to the fire, examining the large
patch of embers. He scuffed some of the back with his boot,
drew his knife and started to dig until he brought forth a large
ball of what appeared to be mud. Carefully juggling the hot
ball the Kid got it clear of the fire and broke it with the back
of the bowie knife blade. The mud cracked and came away to
expose the plump shape of a wild turkey as big as the one
which was still spluttering and burning on the fire. The dried
mud stripped off all the feathers as it came away and the bird
lay ready for carving and eating.

"I sure could talk about something more cheerful," he told
the watching Vance. "But you being all shot to death like that,
you just wouldn't be interested."

"I'm not that badly hurt," Vance replied. "Besides, turkey's good for a sick man. I had an Uncle Thadeus, he always insisted on eating turkey when he was ill."

The Kid grinned, his razor-edged knife went around and carved a generous slab of breast meat from the bird, then he pulled a twig from the fire, impaled the meat on it and passed it to Vance.

"This's what I call a well cooked bird," the Kid remarked. "And more than enough for us——"

"Yowee! Food!" whooped a voice from the trees and Johnny Raybold appeared, leading the horses.

"You spoke a whole heap too soon, *amigo*," growled Mark disgustedly. "Reckon we could insult him so he'd go away?"

"With *food* here?" Dusty replied. "That's about as likely as finding an honest Ysabel, now isn't it?"

Johnny saw the bandaging attempts and opened his saddle pouch to take out some strips of white cloth. He cast a critical eye around him and remarked: "That was a tolerable amount of shooting for just three dead Apaches."

"There's two more in the bushes," Dusty replied. "We got them all. Settle on down and have some turkey."

"I wouldn't say no," Johnny drawled.

"You've never even tried," growled the Kid.

Dusty waited until Vance's wound was attended to then gave his orders. "Eat up, then I'm riding back to the herd. You come with me, Vance, I want Doc to take a look at that shoulder."

"I just helped with it," Johnny pointed out.

"Sure," agreed Dusty. "That's what I mean."

Stone saw the two men riding towards him, saw Dusty's hat make a wild wave to him and knew everything was all right, except that Vance had his arm in a sling. Sending his horse forward, Stone rode to meet the other two, he glanced at Vance and asked, "Everything all right?"

"Got them all and Vance's our only casualty."

"Head back along the line, Vance," Stone ordered. "Tell Doc to look you over. How about it, Dusty?"

Dusty cast a glance back at the herd and nodded. "They look thirsty enough."

"They're ready for it."

Dusty and Stone had experienced the way of a herd of cattle when it was thirsty and got a scent of water. With luck the cattle would run right through the trees and could be picked up at the edge of the water. There would be some time lost but it would be worth the extra trouble.

"I left Mark, Lon and Johnny to watch out. They've got orders to down any Apache who shows any sign of coming their way, looking for the other scouts."

Time passed and the herd moved on. It had been allowed to graze but now the riders closed in on the flanks, pushing the animals closer together and the pace increased. The previous days had been at a steady drive and without trouble, now the extra pace did not unduly worry them.

Birdie had seen Vance with his arm in the sling but neither fainted nor went into hysterics. She realised that the wound was not over serious or he would hardly have come riding back in such a manner. She left her place on the herd for a few moments just to make sure, then went back to handle her part and follow the lead of Doc Leroy who was called back to check the wound. From then until Doc's return Birdie covered his and her own section of the line. Doc came back after a time, he rode alongside Birdie as she cursed at a steer.

"He'll live," he said cheerfully and raced his horse up the line.

The woods were in sight and the wind was blowing towards the cattle from it. The big lead steer threw back his head, snuffled the air, then lumbered on again for a time. Once more he sniffed as the wind bore the scent of water to him.

"Watch 'em now!" Stone roared. "They've scented the water."

The change in the cattle was instant, heads flung back, snorts rang out and they started to move faster. Stone watched them, not wanting a stampede and not wanting them to run off too much fat in a wild race.

It was now the skill of the cowhands showed itself. They rode like centaurs, keeping the pace of the herd under control. Dusty appeared to be everywhere and wherever Dusty was not Stone Hart was. Riding with the wildest, sending her cow-trained horse into the herd, around it, chasing on the cattle, rode Birdie. This was the chance for her husband's dream to come true and she meant to see that it did.

Now the herd was headed for the woods and Mark Counter boiled up out of the dust to help the others. Johnny and the Kid did not appear, they were well to the north, ready, willing and both very able to handle any chance Apache who came within range of their rifles.

In the woods it was a wild tangle, the riders all took time out to get fresh mounts from the remuda and then charged back. There was no time for refinement or gentle handling, the steers were on the scent of water and headed for it. Not one of the herd had any other thought but to sink his nose into the cool water he could smell ahead. There was no thought of scattering and escape to freedom in the trees, not while thirst ruled.

Full into the water went the leading cattle, pushed on by the steers behind. A big roan longhorn went down, thrashing in the water and risking life and limb. Dusty was after it, his rope flashed out and the huge paint churned wildly as it hauled the steer clear by brute strength alone.

"Just like a herd of women," Stone growled disgustedly, speaking to, without looking back at, the rider behind him.

Something hard thudded into his ribs and he turned to find himself looking into Birdie's laughing eyes. For a moment he flushed red, then he grinned also. The present conditions gave a man no chance at all of feeling embarrassed and he had come to know Birdie quite well on this cattle drive.

"Move them across!" he roared and Birdie was the first to send her horse into the water.

The cattle, those which had drunk their fill already, were eased across the river with little or no trouble. On the other bank the woods were neither so thick nor tempting to the cattle and the herd moved on through them, encouraged by cursing riders. Stone held half the men back to make a search of the woods and the odd strays were picked up, sent over to join the long and winding column of cattle on their way to Tombstone.

The remuda was watered and moved over by Rin and the night hawk, then the two wagons brought across. By this time the day was well advanced and Chow decided to set up his night camp on the river bank. The herd was pushed on for a couple of miles and then salted and allowed to bed down for the night. There was no trouble in getting the cattle to settle down for they were leg weary and the grazing on the bed ground was good. Stone kept his usual double night herd out, for they were not out of danger yet.

There was a light-hearted and happy-go-lucky air about the camp. They were past the most serious danger now, or would be by nightfall tomorrow. Birdie went to the bedwagon and collected a towel, some soap and a change of clothing. She also dug out her husband's razor and clean clothes, strolled over to him and remarked:

"You look like you've spent a week in a hawg-pen. There's all that clean water down there, let's go try some of it."

Birdie and Vance were away a long time. They walked back towards the camp, passing several of the trail crew who were headed upstream to wash the dirt and dust from them. Vance had his good arm around his wife. She smiled up at him.

"Vance honey," she said gently. "Wouldn't it be funny if our first baby got his start on the banks of the Carne River?"

Vance chuckled and squeezed Birdie. "I think it would, anyway, I hope it's a girl."

She looked the cowhands over on their return, remarking they all looked like strangers. This brought Chow in with a growl about them being all right until they had to eat woman's fixings and the feud was started afresh.

Laughing in delight because she'd put one over that Chow couldn't top, Birdie walked away before he could find an answer. She found Doc Leroy sitting on the edge of the bedwagon and joined him. Doc's long, slim and almost boneless looking hands were busy, rolling some cloth to form a bandage.

"Is Vance's shoulder going to be all right?" she asked.

"Sure," Doc replied.

"Where'd you meet up with Dusty first?" she went on, talking because she was too happy and excited to think of sleep.

"Up to Quiet Town, in Montana just after the war. We ran the law there under him. He taught me there's a whole lot more to wearing a badge than hauling a drunk to jail and settling back to take a cut of the fine."

"Is he fast?"

"He's faster than fast and twice as accurate," Doc replied. "Mark's real fast too. They've got a boy rides with them now, he bust his arm and couldn't come with them on this. His name's Waco and he's near on as fast as either of them." Doc chuckled. "I bet young Waco near turned the air blue when he heard he couldn't come. That boy'd walk into a gun, knowing he was going to get killed, if Dusty told him to."

"Dusty's only a small man, I suppose," Birdie remarked thoughtfully. "It's a funny thing though. I can never think of him as being small."

"Neither can I. He stands a full seventeen hands high from where I ride. Put me a choice between him and Stone—well I surely wouldn't want to make a choice."

Birdie sat back. "You handle doctoring real well."

"Sure," Doc answered. "I read medicine for a time. Then my folks were killed in an Indian raid and I lost a brother on one of the early drives with Stone. I was just on eighteen when I left it. I've learned all I could, read books, talked to doctors. One day I'll maybe get a chance and go back to medical school and really be able to put M.D. after my name."

That day came, but it was not for four years and by that time much had changed in the hectic life of Doc Leroy.

Birdie climbed down from the wagon and headed back to her husband. She thought of the men who rode their herd. In the few days she'd come to know them all probably better than she knew her own ranch crew. They were a varied bunch, each man a rugged individualist in his own right, yet they formed a good team, even the new hands taken on in Tombstone just for the drive. The regular Wedge crew were loyal to each other and to their boss. Yet she also felt that a good part of their admiration and loyalty was also given to that small, soft talking, fast moving man from the Rio Hondo, the man called Dusty Fog.

"We're through the worst of it now, aren't we?" she asked squatting cowhand style on her haunches by her husband, Dusty and Stone.

"Just about," Stone replied.

"I still think we'll have to watch ourselves at that draw near Tombstone," Dusty warned. "That'll be Rambeau's first, last and best chance to hit at us."

CHAPTER ELEVEN

Orders From The Syndicate

King Rambeau stamped into the King Saloon in no mood to make conversation or even think of returning the greetings of the bartender who handed him a small and unopened package. It was four days after the death of Iowa Parsons and he was returning from a very unpleasant interview with a leading member of the Syndicate who had come by fast coach from Tucson.

The inquest on Iowa Parsons was long over and the verdict had been brought in "Died of a case of slow", a verdict which had been used more than once on the victims of the killer.

"A kid brought this in while you was out, boss," remarked the bartender.

Rambeau did not need to ask or even think what was in the parcel. It contained the most expensive bracelet he could buy in Tombstone and had been delivered with a note suggesting a meeting, to Cindy Alban. The girl had not even opened the package and the note, torn into pieces, was found inside the envelope, which was stuck to the back.

At any other time this might have driven Rambeau into a rage but not with the worries he had on his mind. The Syndicate man had been brief, brutally brief. Iowa Parsons had been sent to Tombstone to handle trouble at the saloon and the Syndicate wanted to know how he came to be killed. There was no lying or arguing either, the man knew about Rambeau's manipulations, knew that Parsons was breaking one of their strictest rules when he sat in a game which did not concern him.

Stamping up the stairs and opening his room door, Rambeau still could hear the man's cold, impersonal voice:

"You started this game, Rambeau. Now you've got to finish it. The word's all through the Territory that a Syndicate man started in to take over a herd and folks are waiting to see how it goes. You've got to handle that herd, get it one way or another."

To Rambeau's request for more guns the man merely pointed out that there were any amount of men around Tombstone who would be pleased to hire out their skill with a Colt. Not another man would the Syndicate send. They'd lost one of their best and nothing was worse for their kind of business than to have it known their guns were capable of being beaten.

So it all fell on Rambeau. He must succeed or—well, the Syndicate had no use for living failures at whom men who lived under Syndicate inspired terror might point a finger and gain courage by.

"Forget that actress and concentrate on the herd," the Syndicate man had said before dismissing Rambeau with a casual wave of his hand. "You've too much on now to become involved with the likes of her. You can't afford to buy her fancy bracelets. The men you hire to take that herd are going to come out of your end."

That was the first time, although he'd suspected it all along, that Rambeau was sure he was being watched by spies for the Syndicate. He found himself wondering who they might be; the bartender? possibly; any of the dealers. It could be any of the people he employed. Or it might be anyone, for the Syndicate was a large organisation with members in all walks of life.

On the table in Rambeau's room was a carpet-bag. He glanced at the bag, not knowing what it was, then realising it would be Iowa Parsons' belongings, released to his ownership. He did not know if there was anyone who might want the killer's belongings and was about to sweep the bag to the floor when he realised that Parsons was a frugal man who never spent money if he could help it. The man was one of the best paid guns of the Syndicate and his fees for killing ran to four figures. He might have banked his money, if so there could be a clue to where the money was. Rambeau needed money, for his share of the profits would hardly cover what he would need to pay out to get the herd.

Tipping the bag upside down over his bed Rambeau allowed the contents to fall out. There was little enough, a change of underclothing, a new shirt, two boxes of bullets, one for the .45 Colt revolver, the other .41 Remington rimfire loads, and a wooden box.

Rambeau was about to sweep the articles back into the bag and toss it out of the room when a thought struck him. He lifted up the box and opened the lid, hoping to find some hint as to where Parsons stashed his money. Inside was nothing of the kind. The box contained only two things. One was a Remington double derringer, the weapon the second box of bullets would be used for. The other object appeared to be a type of card hold-out machine. Rambeau knew something of card hold-outs, they were made to be strapped to the wrist and by an arrangement of springs would catapult the held-out cards into the palm. Rambeau ignored the hold-out for a moment, then a thought struck him. Parsons would never risk any of his money on gambling, in fact, never played any gambling games and so would have no need for the hold-out.

It was then that Rambeau saw the clip, instead of the usual shape, being wide enough to hold the desired playing cards, was made in the shape of a U, just large enough to grip the barrels of that derringer.

Quickly Rambeau removed his coat and dropped it on to the bed, then turned up the cuff on his right shirt sleeve and fixed on the straps of the hold-out. He took up the derringer and clipped it into the restraining U. Then he opened his wardrobe door and faced the full length mirror. Pressing his arm against his side he saw the derringer jerk forward. It did not quite reach his palm so he adjusted the hold-out lower. This time the squat little weapon came correctly into his palm. It arrived in a split second and he brought it up and lined. That was fast, almost as fast as the way that small Texan drew his guns.

Turning down the shirt sleeve after setting the gun again Rambeau donned his jacket and then tried the hold-out. There was no pause as the derringer flashed into his hand and lined again. That was just what he needed, a secret, hidden weapon which could be produced with the speed that these fast men drew their Colts.

Going down the stairs once more Rambeau halted and looked around. Two of his men lounged at the bar, the two who had been with him earlier that week when he tried in the barber's shop to force Vance Brownlow to his will. They caught their boss's nod and came forward, falling in behind him like courtiers following their liege lord. Where he was going they did not know, what he was going to do was not yet explained to them, but they followed him.

Cindy Alban and Miles Hamish followed their usual route from the boarding house in the respectable part of Tombstone to the theatre, where they were due to rehearse their new play. They had to pass through one of the rougher sections of town to reach the theatre but so far had met with nothing but friendly nods and politeness.

In the few days since her arrival Cindy had become well known in Tombstone and well liked. Her songs, her pathetic actions as the poor, down-trodden heroine of some tear-jerking drama, met with almost universal approval. She brought with her a nostalgic note of home, the comfort of a good woman, to men who saw little of female company and less of good women. Of all the men of the town only King Rambeau showed any sign of having designs on her virtue. He was the type of villain which nightly met his well-deserved fate at the hands of the handsome hero, Cindy mused, although he was by far more dangerous, for his threat was real.

"I was always taught never to escort the same lady twice

running," Miles Hamish remarked with a smile at the girl. "This makes the fourth day, doesn't it?"

"It does," she answered. "You'll be having me think it is something serious soon, Miles?"

"Don't you think it is?"

Cindy was aobut to make a reply when she saw the three men who came from a sidestreet and stood blocking the sidewalk. Her fingers bit into Hamish's arm. "Miles, look! It's Rambeau."

Hamish looked forward, saw the way the men stood and knew there was likely to be trouble. The young actor was neither a coward nor a rash fool. He could handle himself in a rough-house brawl but he knew he would have no chance against three men. He also knew Rambeau meant to force his attentions on the girl and could not stand by watching it.

"Hello, songbird," Rambeau said, nodding as the man and girl approached. "I sent you a letter and present."

"Which I returned to you," Cindy answered. "I'm not interested in you or your presents, now I'd like to come past, please."

"Is that so?" Rambeau sneered, then his eyes went to Hamish. "You're not saying much, play-actor. Maybe you're not so much of a hero off the stage."

"Send your two men away and we'll see about it."

Rambeau grinned. "Hear that, boys. The play-actor's getting all uppish. He needs taking down some, doesn't he?"

"We could handle him I reckon, boss," said the taller man, a tough, who was known by the name of Dutchy Schwarz in Tombstone.

"You know, I reckon we could," Rambeau agreed. "Let's see."

Hamish pushed Cindy aside and the girl moved clear, having more sense than get in his way when he would need every chance to move freely. Her eyes went to the three men as they moved towards Hamish. She thought of running for help, but knew that before she could get to the theatre and bring back Joe Raymond and a couple of stagehands it would be too late. Miles Hamish would be battered into a bloody wreck and never able to play a hero again.

"Three to one. Now that's what I call good odds."

The words were spoken from an alley nearby and brought the attention of the entire group to it. Standing with one shoulder resting against the wall was a thin, sallow man in gambler's dress but with the butt of a ten gauge shot pistol showing from under the left side of his coat, where it was held in a shoulder clip.

The three men halted their advance. They froze like rabbits when faced by a weasel and the description was very apt for that thin man was Doc Holliday and his reputation built him to be every bit as wild and dangerous as any weasel.

"Are you cutting in, Holliday?" Rambeau asked.

"Now that's a good question," came the mocking reply. "Make your play and find out, one way or the other."

Rambeau felt scared and could almost feel the fear in his men. They might chance stacking against Doc Holliday in a pinch, or when primed for it by bottled brave-maker. They were neither primed, nor fighting drunk right now and they were not willing to match shots with Holliday. He was a dying man, they knew that, his life meant nothing to him, or so rumour had it. A man did not stack against someone who was not worried if he lived or died, without great provocation, or great risk. There was another thing stopping those hired guns. The shot pistol Holliday carried had only two barrels but each barrel carried a deadly nine-buckshot charge which would tear a man in half at close range. He would certainly get one of them, possibly both. If a survivor killed Holliday he would be no better case for he would have the Earp brothers hunting him to avenge the killing of their friend.

"Reckon you boys have business some other place, haven't you?" Holliday asked coldly, his eyes flickering to the two gunmen.

The two men licked their lips and glanced nervously at their boss. For a moment Rambeau thought of using his wrist holstered derringer, then a nagging doubt hit him. He was far from the East and in New York the gangster's weapons were his hands, feet, a club, a knife, or a set of Tammany mittens, as knuckledusters were called. The gun had little or no use in the work of the New York crook and Rambeau was such a man.

He had made the incredible blunder of not checking to see if the derringer was loaded. If he started to draw and the weapon was empty he would be dead before he even knew it, for there would be no hesitation in the way Holliday acted.

"Clear the sidewalk, all of you."

There was no mild request in Holliday's words. It was an order and one which only a roaring Colt could refuse to obey.

"Do you want to hold his men off my back, Doc?" Hamish inquired, for he knew Holliday, having been introduced at a party given in the show's honour by a prominent Law and Order Party member.

"I'm doing it for the young lady, not for you, Hamish," Holliday answered. "I reckon a fist fight might be amusing, but she doesn't want her hero with his face all marked up."

"Please, Miles," gasped Cindy urgently, gripping the actor's arm once more.

Hamish wanted to stay behind and try conclusions with Rambeau, to prove to the girl that he could handle things off-stage as well as on. Yet he knew that Rambeau would go all out to damage his face and he did have the show to consider. Without Hamish to play the hero roles Madame Paula would be in trouble. Regretfully, dealing with Rambeau must be postponed until some later date.

Rambeau and his men cleared the sidewalk and Cindy took Hamish's arm, forcing him by the other men. Holliday stood as he had all the time, his sallow face showing nothing of what he thought.

"The actor might find himself a shy girl one of these days," Rambeau snarled, watching the man and girl walk away.

Holliday's lips drew back in a cold smile like the death's head grin as his tallon-like right hand lifted towards the butt of his shot pistol and for a moment Rambeau thought he'd gone too far.

"You've got a yeller streak, King!" purred Holliday, his eyes catching the fear which flickered across the saloon-keeper's face. "Now listen to me, and listen real good. If anything happens to that girl, or the actor, I'll kill you on sight. Just remember, anything at all. You can take my word on it."

Rambeau looked at the thin face and read death on it. Any

attempt at revenge on either the girl or the actor would have to wait now. Holliday was a strange man and might easily forget the stand he'd taken in a few days' time.

For all that, in the days which followed, Rambeau found a cooling air in the way the Earps acted towards him. No longer was his saloon on their list of places to stop for drinks. There was a different air around the town too, the men who had backed away from Rambeau as a Syndicate man now grew bold again.

There was another problem facing Rambeau. He could not get men to handle the stealing of the herd. The hired guns who hung around Tombstone grew evasive or even disdainful when he asked them. Those hired fighting men knew the reputation of the Wedge trail crew and more, they knew the reputation of the three men from the Rio Hondo country who rode with the cattle.

It was a worrying time for Rambeau. He had the contract for the sale of the herd arranged; they would be driven to a small place near Tombstone and butchered by skilled men, then the meat sold in town. The end was prepared, there only remained the most vital detail, getting hold of the herd.

It was two days before the herd was due to arrive and Rambeau still had not managed to hire the men he so urgently needed. He was worried as there had been a cold warning from the Syndicate. They were having trouble, people were sitting back and waiting for the first failure of a Syndicate man's project. It could break them if he failed to get the herd. Yet for all that they still could not supply him with gunmen, they needed every man they could lay hands on to hold down the restless spirits on whom they preyed.

At noon Rambeau entered his saloon after a fruitless morning looking for men. He was crossing towards the stairs when he saw a tallish, round-shouldered and prematurely bald man sitting with back to the wall. The man looked up, a cold grin on his Indian dark face as the saloon-keeper approached.

"Howdy, Burt," Rambeau greeted. "Are you working?"

"Depends on what," replied Burt Alvord.

"Something that will pay well."

"Sorry, King, that's not my line," growled the dark man.

"I don't know if the herd got through the Apaches, but knowing the men who're driving it I'd bet they did. In that case I'm not stacking up against them."

Rambeau felt cold disappointment. Burt Alvord was a man well fancied by some for the two shooting matches. He'd been a fast-gun deputy with a reputation for bringing in dead prisoners. He was known to have contacts on both sides of the border and of either steering a wanted man across, or killing him for the reward on his dead body.

Taking out his wallet, Rambeau said, "No hard feelings, Burt."

"Could put you in the way of somebody who might take on."

"Who?"

"How much?—Then who."

Rambeau looked at the Indian dark face and felt anger. There was only one of two ways to deal with a man like Burt Alvord. Pay him or kill him. Rambeau had the sleeve-hidden derringer loaded now but he did not intend using it.

"That depends on what you have to offer."

Alvord grinned. "Say a dozen bad-hat Mormons who need money to skip the border. I stood to gain on them one way or the other. Figured to win a hundred at your poker table tonight. I'll lose that if I go for them."

"Fifty down and fifty when the men show."

"Don't be a piker, King," Alvord purred. "Make it an even hundred now and the same when I bring Pilbourne in. There, I've given you that much."

Rambeau frowned. He'd heard of Pilbourne. The man was wanted, badly wanted, by the Elders of the Mormon Church. He was a bad Mormon who'd robbed and killed Gentile men and stolen their livestock. This was not regarded as too serious a crime in the Mormon book, but he'd killed an Elder of their church and looted the church funds.

"You couldn't find him, King," Alvord warned, seeing the expression which crossed the other man's face. "And I'd surely take it unkind on any man who tried."

"I want them tonight at the latest."

"That could cost you more money, but I'll be generous,"

Alvord answered. "I'll have him here by ten o'clock."

Rambeau watched the other man slouch away, then went up to his room. He took a map from the desk and spread it out. It was an Army survey map of the area around Tombstone and he ran his finger along a pencilled line from the Carne River to the town. He tapped the X Parsons made on the map when they first planned this business. The original plan had been to allow Brownlow to run his herd alone, then hit it and wipe out the trail crew at the draw near Tombstone, well beyond the area where a large band of Apaches might be expected. They planned that first, then to force the rancher to take them in as partners. This was their second plan, allow the herd to reach the draw and ambush it, wiping out Brownlow and his crew.

The rest of the day dragged by and Rambeau had little interest in anything which happened in his place. A miner hit a lucky streak on the roulette wheel, a streak so lucky that it licked even the crooked wheel which ran a large percentage for the house. Normally Rambeau would have either steered the man out, or arranged for him to wake up in some dark alley with his pockets emptied. Tonight Rambeau did not even give the man a second glance.

Sharp at ten o'clock Alvord arrived. He was alone and Rambeau felt a momentary annoyance, then realised that a man like Pilbourne would never show himself in a saloon, especially a well-known one in Tombstone.

"Go in the back room, King," Alvord said. "Hand me the hundred now, open the back door and he's waiting out there."

Rambeau handed over the hundred dollars, turned and went into the back room. He opened the door and for an instant thought Alvord had robbed him. Then a man stepped into the light, a big, gaunt, whiskered man in a dirty black suit and with a low tied Colt at his side. He came into the room with a wolf-cautious step, but shook his head when Rambeau went to close the door.

"I've two men out there," warned the gaunt man. "They are stood so they can cover all the room."

"I'm not armed," Rambeau answered, showing his gunless sides. "Take a seat and I'll pour you a drink. You're Pilbourne, are you?"

"I am."

"Can your men all handle guns—and cattle?"

"We have often handled both."

"Then I want you to dress as Apaches. I've got clothing stashed away that'll fit your men, and I want you to hit a trail herd of about five hundred head. You'll have to kill all the men and a woman who are riding with it. Make it look like real Apache work."

"Just that?" asked Pilbourne. "Why can't you get men from town to handle it?"

"Because the herd's being handled by the Wedge. You've maybe heard of them. And riding with it are Dusty Fog, Mark Counter and the Ysabel Kid."

"They are men I've heard of. All can handle their weapons well and it will not be easy to take them."

"The way I plan it they *will* be easy," Rambeau answered. "It's near enough to Tombstone for you to hit them when they're relaxed and thinking they're safe and far enough out for the shooting not to be heard and attract attention."

"In that case what's to stop me and my men just hitting this herd for ourselves?" asked Pilbourne.

"You don't know where to hit, for one thing. For another, not even the Clantons could pay you as well as I can. You don't know anyone in town who would take it off your hands and it is here in Tombstone the money's to be made. I'll give you a thousand dollars and the same to be split among your men if you pull it off."

"Do you know when the herd is coming?"

"Neither when nor if," Rambeau admitted. "The Apaches may have got it, although I'd bet that crew could get through. But at latest it should be coming through the draw I'll point out on the map in two days' time. I'll make an agreement with you. If the herd comes through and you get it before the Fair I'll pay you what I said. If it hasn't got through I'll pay Alvord to get you and your men out of the country. If it comes through after the County Fair is over, which isn't likely, then you can have it and sell it for what you can get."

"I want that in writing," Pilbourne replied.

It was some moments before Rambeau would agree to put his name to anything so incriminating, but he gave in at last.

This was his only chance, his last hope of getting the herd. He took out a sheet of paper, a pen and ink, from a desk in the table. The back room was used for big stake poker games and writing materials were often needed when some player ran out of ready cash and wished to give a note on a bet. The letter Rambeau wrote would be enough to hang him and might leave him open to blackmail later, but he doubted it. Pilbourne and his men were fleeing from something more deadly than United States law, they were fleeing from the Danites, the dreaded Avenging Angels, the police, regulators and avengers of the Mormon people. Once this business was over Pilbourne and his men would make the most of their time heading for the comparative safety of the Mexican border.

"Where are the clothes?" Pilbourne asked, folding the sheet of paper and sliding it into a special slot between the leather and lining of his riding boot.

"I've got them in a trunk up in my room. We can get them without going through the saloon. I'll tell you where to deliver the cattle. I'll leave the money waiting for you there and I'll want that letter back then."

It was midnight before Pilbourne left, but he had a clear plan laid out for him, one he could follow. Rambeau was contented as he went to bed that night.

The following day there was excitement for a soldier, riding despatch between two of the Forts, came into Tombstone with word that he'd seen a trailherd. From what the soldier said Rambeau guessed the herd would be arriving at the draw the following day. His main plans were all made, a fast horse ready to take him with all the money he could get down below the border before the Syndicate could know he was planning a doublecross. There was only one thing left to do. He called in all the hired men of the saloon and told them he expected trouble that night and they would, on pain of offending the Syndicate, back him in it. Lastly he called aside Dutchy Schwarz and the other man and offered them a sizeable chunk of money to do something for him.

There was a hard and evil grin on Rambeau's face as he sat waiting for the night which should bring him word that the herd was in Pilbourne's hands and his money was on its way. It would bring something more. He took a sheet of paper from the desk in his room and wrote a letter which would bring Miles Hamish forth to a murderous beating and leave him disfigured for life and would also bring the girl Cindy Alban into his clutches. He would leave Tombstone with something to remember the name King Rambeau.

CHAPTER TWELVE

At the Draw

"Damn the heat, the flies, this stinking stain, everything!"

Pilbourne looked at the speaker with a cold, grim expression on his face. He and all his men wore the trade shirts, buckskin trousers and headbands of Apaches, with long lank black wigs and dark stain adding to the picture they made. They were lying in whatever shade they could find, all eyes on the rolling dust cloud which was coming closer all the time. It didn't look like a whole lot of dust for five hundred head, Pilbourne thought, but he did not know for sure what the country was like out there.

The draw through which the herd must pass lay below Pilbourne and his men. There was a flat and open trail running down the centre of the draw, but on either side of it rocks and scrubby bushes offered good cover. The slopes rose up on either side, in some places gently, in others sheer and steep. Pilbourne's men were halfway down one of the more gentle parts, an area which offered good cover to them and places where they could lay concealed, their rifles lining on the trail. He'd split his gang into two parts, one at either side of the trail, the

143

men taking up fighting positions ready, each picking his own in a way which showed they knew what they were doing. The herd would be well within the killing area, the cowhands holding the cattle bunched and so would be under the guns. Pilbourne's men were fair shots and could be expected to cut down the cowhands in one roaring volley. The herd would break, stampede, but Pilbourne had told half of his men to run for horses as soon as the cattle broke. The horses, up over the rims, tethered and waiting, would be grabbed by three men from either side and sent after the herd. The remaining men would deal with any of the trail crew who might have been missed by the first volley.

There was a cold, cruel and efficient way about Pilbourne's plan, he took no chances and was callous as to the fact that he might cause the death of a dozen men and a woman. They meant nothing to him, nothing more than a thousand dollars with which to get well clear of the vengeance of the Danites.

"Stop whining," he snarled at the man. "I feel those things as you do. This is far better than facing the wrath of the Danites, isn't it?"

"It is," the man agreed. "With the money for those cattle I will go south and make sure they do not find me."

"Then stop whining," snarled Pilbourne.

"What of the horse I thought I heard in the night?" asked the man worriedly.

Pilbourne looked across at the other men with cold eyes. They made camp in a bosque near the draw and the previous night this man, while on sentry, had wakened the others, saying he thought he'd heard a horse moving in the darkness. There had been no sound to greet the ears of the others and they tended to scoff at the idea.

"You were either hearing things, or it was a stray," Pilbourne replied. He looked to where the dust was getting very close, although there was still no sign of the men who handled the herd. "Get to your place and I will find mine."

Over the bank the other men were moving into their places ready. Pilbourne darted to a place where the cliff rose steep for a way and underneath the shelter offered by the slope were two rocks behind which he might hide and fire his rifle in some safety.

Nearer the dust rolled, vague shapes showing in it where men rode the herd and kept them coming. Pilbourne was not a man who had done much work with cattle, no matter what his boast to Rambeau had been. He'd worked on a Mormon farm and his knowledge of legitimate cattle herding had been gained with slow and docile milk-cows. His other knowledge of cattle herding had been on the wrong side of the law, when speed was of an urgent necessity if a man did not want to feel the hairy touch of a hangman's noose around his neck. So Pilbourne saw nothing unusual in the speed the dust cloud was approaching and did not think it strange a herd of cattle being taken to a legitimate market was getting pushed too fast.

Now the cattle were near the opening of the draw, or those dust wrapped shapes were. The ground was hard and stony here and as Pilbourne opened his mouth to let out a wild Indian yell to alert his men the "cattle" came into view from the dust.

Pilbourne's hands gripped his rifle, sighting it down ready to tumble the point rider nearest to him. His finger rested lightly on the Winchester's trigger and was about to squeeze when he saw—and so did every one of his men—that no cattle were running from the dust cloud. Only horses, riderless horses, streaming along. Of the men who drove the herd there was no sight at the moment.

"It's a trick!" screamed one of the men, rearing up into view and waving his rifle. "They're——"

That was his last word alive. Johnny Raybold came out of the dust cloud, towing a heavy weighted sack from his saddle. Once more they'd proved that dust had its use and Pilbourne's men fell for it as had the Apache braves. Johnny gave no time to gloating over the success of the trick. His Winchester rifle was in his shoulder even while his big horse ran at full speed. The rifle cracked and the exposed man went over backwards, a bullet in his head.

Even before the draw threw back echoes of the rifle shot Johnny had unshipped from the saddle of his racing horse and lit down running. He hit the ground behind a rock, his rifle coming out to make another man duck back before he could send a bullet at the other riders.

The horses, the herd's remuda, went on, coming out of the dust cloud where it ended on the hard ground. Rusty Willis,

Doc Leroy and two of the new hands were with the horses,
each man dismounting as fast as he could. One of the new
hands was not quite fast enough. Pilbourne and his men were
over their surprise and the rifles bellowed out. The cowhand
was leaping from his horse when lead caught him and he seemed
to collapse in mid air, his body hitting the dirt of the trail rolling
and then laying limp against a rock. Doc and the others made
it to the rocks by the side of the trail, flattening down and
waiting for their chance. They'd heard the wild war yell, seen
the Indian-like shapes and thought Apaches were attacking
them. This gave them little worry, for they could see this was
only a small band and their escape through the encircling Apache
net made them a little contemptuous of the much-vaunted
Apaches.

It was at that moment they saw that there was an urgent
need for them to shoot and shoot accurately.

In the rear of the herd, wild with excitement, rode young
Rin, the wrangler. In the heat of the moment, carried away by
the wild ride through the dust and out into danger, the boy
forgot, or ignored, every order Dusty Fog had given him the
previous day. Rin should have turned his horse, racing it up
the slope and around, clear of the shooting beyond the top of
the rim, then come down and picked up the racing remuda
when they tired from their run.

Now was long past the moment when he should have turned
for, whooping like an Indian, flattened along the neck of his
horse, fanning its ears with his hat and working his Kelly
petmaker spurs like wild, he sent his horse after the remuda.
Rin was young, not yet having reached his sixteenth birthday.
On the last drive north with Stone a bunch of Osaga renegades
tried to run off the remuda. Rin turned, drew his old Navy
Colt and charged the men even before Johnny, Rusty and Doc
came sweeping back to aid him. He'd fired three wild shots
and before his three friends opened fire, saw one dirty, vermin
crawling Indian go backwards from his horse. Rin knew in that
moment he'd had his man for breakfast. He'd ridden away
from the herd and been violently sick after that, but his courage
was untouched by the incident. Courage or pure blind wildness
it might have been, putting himself out like that. He did not
know which it was, only that he did not intend to allow the

remuda to scatter if he could help it.

Lead slapped the air and whistled around Rin as he rode. Johnny was on his feet, racing forward, his rifle crashing as he darted from cover to cover, trying to save the wild and reckless boy. The others all fired fast too. The men on the slopes were all shooting, throwing lead and it seemed that some of it must catch.

It did.

Johnny jerked under the impact of a bullet, staggered and crashed down into the hard ground. He fell in plain view but was still alive, as showed in the way he tried to crawl to some kind of safety and avoid the lead which kicked up dust and dirt spurts around him. Pilbourne and his men saw the cowhand was wounded, saw they had no chance of getting the fast riding boy who was now through their ambush and streaking after the remuda like the devil hunting down a yearling. So the rifles were turned to make an end of the wounded man and cut down any man who tried to help him.

Everything was in favour of Pilbourne and his men now. They had the others under the guns and were preparing to make the most of it. Already one of the cowhand bunch, Rusty Willis, was darting forward to try and rescue his friend. He should make the next victim. The herd would be coming along, short-handed and could still be taken. Everything was in favour of the Mormons? or so Pilbourne thought, and it was a good thought.

Yet it was not correct.

Dusty Fog, Mark Counter and the Ysabel Kid came into view on the rim above Pilbourne. They came riding their big stallions and each held a saddlegun in his hands as he came into sight.

Dusty had known men were waiting at the draw, known it because the Ysabel Kid had seen their camp and only the alert ears of the sentry prevented his getting in close enough to know more of the waiters. He'd not taken any chances, but had slipped away in Indian silence and warned Dusty, who laid on this surprise move. That it had cost one man his life was not Dusty's fault.

The Kid's old yellow boy rifle flowed to his shoulder and spat out, lancing flame down towards the valley. The bullet caught one of the watching men between the shoulder blades and tossed his lifeless body forward on to the rocks.

Dusty and Mark sent their horses down the slope in a wild sliding run that would have unseated a lesser rider. They were cavalrymen in training and their belief was that the best way to take an enemy was charge him while he was unprepared.

Down the slope they came, the Kid following them on foot, sending the big white stallion back over the rim to safety. Yet even as he ran the Kid kept up a rapid and accurate fire which did much to save Johnny's life, for no man before the Kid dare stay up long enough to take a careful aim. Then the Kid found a spot and came to a halt. His pants pockets bulged with fodder for his old rifle as he forced the flat-nosed .44 bullets through the loading slot and fired again with barely a pause.

The surprise attack from above shook Pilbourne and his men, but they rallied quickly to it. So far only one of the six on Pilbourne's side was dead, having been caught by the Kid's bullet. The rest turned their attention to the attackers from above them.

Dusty saw a man come up from behind a rock, saw the Sharps carbine as the man brought it up. Dusty left his saddle, hit the ground running, went over a rock in a diving roll. He heard the crash of the Sharps and the impact as the lead hit the rock over which he'd just dived. Dusty ended his roll on his feet and the Winchester carbine spat, held hip high. The man with the Sharps spun around even as he opened the breech to insert a fresh load.

Swinging from the hips, Dusty levered another bullet into the carbine's breech and threw a fast shot which dusted stone chips into the face of a Mormon who showed himself in an attempt to throw down on Mark.

Mark left his saddle and the big blood bay went on down the slope as its rider hit the ground. Following Dusty's paint, the stallion turned back up the slope and over the top and slowed down, joining the Kid's white and waiting for its master. Mark, however, was laying behind a rock and shooting at the men across the valley as he saw they were trying to get Rusty in his attempt to save Johnny.

The Kid's rifle suddenly beat out a tattoo, blazing as fast

as he could work the lever and take a fresh sight. One of his shots, thrown at a man on the opposite slope, caused the same man to rear up. Below, Mark's sighting eye lined on the man, trigger finger squeezed and the Model 78 Winchester kicked back hard. The man's upwards jerk changed direction as the .44.40 bullet struck him and he went down once more.

In rushes from rock to rock Rusty made for Johnny. He hurdled one rock and went rolling over another, flattened for an instant behind yet a third, then darted forward to pull Johnny back behind the largest rock, into a place where he was out of danger from the rifles above him. Rusty knew, even though only a matter of a couple of minutes had elapsed, that he owed his life to the Kid's riflework. There had been times when lead sang close to him and he knew that but for the Kid spoiling any chance of a careful aim the lead would have been much closer.

Even as Rusty brought Johnny to safety there was another man moving in. It was Doc Leroy, his jacket pockets carrying his simple surgical tools and some bandages. At times like this, when going into a fight, Doc always went prepared for any wounds which might come his way. He knew Johnny was in need of his help and was going to do what he could.

Looking around, Rusty saw Doc coming and knew there would not be room for all three of them behind the rock. So without a word he hurled from cover and went racing along through the gauntlet of fire again. Just ahead the side of the draw rose sheer and there was something of an overhang which would shield him from the men on that side, while a rocky ridge would give him shelter from the others. Rusty made it, diving the last few feet and landing in comparative safety, then rolled over to fire up the slope. He could see Mark, Dusty and the Kid, lifted his hand in a cheery wave and jerked it down as a bullet slapped the rock near to it.

Behind the rocks Doc Leroy was working fast. He cut the cloth away from around the wound, cleaned the blood as best he could and grunted. Johnny was still alive, which meant the bullet had not pierced anything vital. Doc knew much about the care and attention of gunshot wounds and he used every bit of skill he possessed now.

"How is he, Doc?" yelled the second of the new hands as he fired up the slope. "We'll rip the heart out of those red devils if he dies."

Doc, never too amiable while working, growled out a curse and ignored the question. Right now he was too busy, his thin, seemingly boneless hands working fast as he probed for the bullet. He found the hardness with the tip of the probe and with care opened the gripping end. The probe had been made on his special design for just such work and he felt the ends close on the bullet. Carefully he drew back. A moan from the now unconscious Johnny brought an end to the movement. Doc was sweating but cool enough. He waited until Johnny was still again, then withdrew the bullet. Not until then did Doc breathe a sigh of relief. Johnny was far from being safe yet, but he was better off now the lead was out of him.

Rusty Willis, in his place under the slope, was worried as to how Johnny was, but he knew better than bother Doc with questions at such a time. His eyes scanned the slope, picking out where Dusty, Mark and the Kid were and spotting the remaining "Apaches". They were now exercising some caution and he could not get a clear shot at any of them.

One of the men above Rusty started to make a careful advance down the slope, sliding from cover to cover like a buck Apache. So good was he and so close the cover, that he had made a considerable distance before any of the men on the other slope saw him. The Kid was first. He saw a splash of colour where no such colour should be. It was only there for an instant, then gone, but that was long enough and more to alert a man as keen sighted as the Ysabel Kid. Now the Kid's rifle was silent. He ignored the slap of a bullet into the rock close to him as he concentrated on that splash of colour and what caused it.

The crawling man was almost on the overhang before he gave the Kid a a chance to do anything. Even then there was little to aim at. There was enough for the Kid to send a bullet whistling at and the lead struck close. The man gave a yell, rolled himself over the rock and down the slope.

Rusty saw dirt, then small rocks trickling over the edge of the overhang, he saw a shape falling and dust got into his eyes, partially blinding him. The man fell, turned in the air, and lit down on his feet. His rifle crashed and the bullet sent chips splattering Rusty's face. Rusty flung himself to one side, his Winchester held in his right hand. The rifle crashed and the butt lashed back to hit hard into Rusty's side. The bullet caught the man under the chin, angled up and burst out of the top of his head, sending the long black wig and headband flying.

Up until that moment Rusty and the other cowhands had believed they were fighting Apaches. Even the Kid did not know for sure they were not, although something had been nagging at his thoughts as he shot. Rusty saw the man reeling back, saw the wig go flying and the band of white skin where the dye had not covered.

"A stinking renegade!"

So excited and annoyed was Rusty that he exposed himself and then flopped back as a bullet grazed his neck. He felt something hot running down under his collar even as he hit the ground.

"Renegades!" Dusty barked to Mark.

"I thought they handled the ambush bad for Apaches," Mark called back. "We'd best show them!"

Not even a bad Apache was hated as was a renegade, a man who raided dressed as an Indian. The renegade could never feel safe in his disguise, for the hand of white and red men was against them. Only the most cold-blooded and murderous outlaw would adopt such tactics and to such a man no mercy was shown.

"I got it," whooped the Kid, as he also watched the man reel back and lose his wig. "I knew there was something wrong. That bunch're all wearing boots."

The Kid had been worried by some nagging doubt from the start of the fight. The men looked like Apaches, from what he could see of them, yet some instict, some stirring of his wild Comanche blood, insisted that these men were not Indians. Now he could see clearly what it was. The Apache would take many things from a white-eye as war trophy and for use. He would take a hat, a shirt, perhaps a set of pants, even underwear. He would take any kind of rifle and sing praises to his Gods all night if the rifle was a Winchester. He would take a revolver and a gunbelt to wear it on. He would not take a pair of boots. They were something he had no use for and would never wear. A white man's boots were useless to the Apache, too noisy for his silent way of moving.

Pilbourne looked around him, saw the last man on his side of the draw crumple over and go down. Then he looked up and saw a larger cloud of dust was approaching. There was no doubt what the dust was caused by. It was the herd and with it rode reinforcements for these cowhands.

The Mormons, on the opposite slope, saw it, those who were able to see anything. That was all they needed to see and started to back away up the slope. Only two made it, passing over the slope fast, the others were still shapes on the ground or moving in their last throes, for from their cover only their heads showed and a hit was likely to prove fatal.

Dusty saw the men go and saw a danger in their going. They'd lost out here and were running, but they might come on young Rin with the remuda. The boy alone would be a good target for the hate and the horses make up in loot for the herd which was safe from them.

"Lon!" Dusty barked. "Take out after Rin and the remuda!"

The Kid gave a wave and started to move back. It was lucky he was always cautious and did not expose himself any more than he needed. Even so, the damage was serious when it came.

Pilbourne found he'd made a basic and deadly dangerous mistake. The place he picked for the fight gave him real good cover, but there was only one way out of it. And covering that escape route were two men who had already showed they could call down their shots with accuracy. He was trapped, the only ways left out were surrender and a certain hanging or fight to the death and try to take as many of them as possible with him. With the wolf-savage hate and lust for killing which drove him on to the outlaw trails, Pilbourne picked the latter way. He saw that black-dressed boy who handled the rifle so well, saw him for an instant, brought up his rifle and took a fast shot.

Fast taken or not, the shot came as close to taking the Kid's life as a man needed and caused more concern to the Kid than a wound would have. The Kid felt a sudden jarring shock and the rifle, the old yellow boy, was torn from his hands. He saw the gun hit the ground and dived forward, scooping it up in passing. Landing in the open, he rolled fast, felt lead strike just behind him and was in cover again.

One look was all the Kid needed to tell him the rifle was finished. The old yellow boy, one of the first of the model which came to be known as the 1866, had come to him just after the war when he first joined Dusty Fog in his quest to bring back Bushrod Sheldon from Mexico. Since then the rifle had never left the Kid, had been in his saddleboot or his hands ready for use. He knew that rifle, knew how it threw at ranges beyond anything the light load of the bullet was meant to be reliable at. Now it was gone, smashed by a bullet which had wrecked the breech mechanism.

The Kid might have been thankful the bullet wrecked his rifle instead of his body, but he was not. All too well the Kid knew the calibre of the men he would be matched against in the Tombstone Rifle Shoot. They were men who knew their rifles as he knew his, men capable of calling down their shots with an accuracy that the Kid would find hard to equal with a new weapon in his hands.

Cold rage gripped the Kid and it took all his self-control to prevent a wild rage-filled rush towards where Pilbourne was hidden. Then sanity came back and he knew that he must get after the remuda. Without his rifle he was of no use against the men in his defensive position and Dusty could far better deal with the man. So the Kid turned and went up the slope, went fast and keeping in cover, for he'd seen how well this renegade could shoot.

Passing over the ridge, the Kid gave a whistle and his white stallion loped back to him. He caught the saddlehorn and swung astride in a lithe Indian-like bound. Turning the white stallion, he headed along the rim over the draw to where he could get down to the bottom in safety and head after the horses. There was anger in his heart, anger and disappointment, for his chances of winning that magnificent "One of a Thousand" Winchester were well below the odds of three to one the bartender at the Bucket of Blood first started him.

The Kid found Rin three miles down the trail. The youngster had caught up with the fleeing horses and now had them under control. He was allowing them to graze and settle down and rode eagerly to where the Kid approached.

"Did we get 'em, Kid?" he whooped excitedly.

"Some of them, boy," answered the Kid. "Why in hell didn't

you go around them like Dusty told you?"

"Shucks, it was quicker the way I come and they didn't hit me."

For a moment the Kid felt anger and almost knocked the boy from his saddle. Then the anger went. Rin was young, wild, reckless, but young. He'd sand to burn and that should never be held against any youngster. Johnny was hit bad but could just have easily have taken the lead in the normal course of the attack. It would do no good to blame Rin for it.

"That's right," he growled. "*They* didn't hit you. But Dusty's going to whale the tar out of you when he lays hands on you."

Rin grinned. The prospect of a hiding did not worry him any. He'd been chapped, held across the wagon tail and had a pair of bull-hide chaps applied to his pants seat without yelling; that had been when he grew slack and nearly lost the remuda in a drive. He reckoned he could take another chapping for the risk he'd run by not following orders.

The Kid sat his big white for a moment, then came to his feet, standing on the saddle to scan the surrounding country. He could see no sign of the two fleeing renegades and guessed they would be headed for the border as fast as their horses carried them. They had seen their gang cut down by the guns of the Texas trail crew. They wanted only to get out of this country and would not bother the remuda.

"We going back to the herd, Kid?" Rin asked.

"Start the remuda back slow, boy," answered the Kid. "I'm headed on to Tombstone. Tell Dusty I've gone to see if I can get another yellow boy."

Without knowing what the Kid was doing, Dusty got down to the business of dislodging Pilbourne from behind the rocks. In this Dusty was acting in the manner of a trained lawman, not as a cowhand. There was a cold determination about the way Dusty flattened down behind a large rock and glanced at Mark. They had been in the same position before and not just the once.

Rusty and the other cowhand made their way up the slope in darting rushes and flattened down near to where Dusty and Mark crouched with their rifles. The cowhand lifted his head and called:

"Dusty, Doc says Johnny'll live."

"Keep down!" Dusty's words cracked like a whip and were echoed by the flat crack of Pilbourne's rifle.

The cowhand flattened down again, his Stetson spinning from his head, so close had the bullet come. A grin came to the man's face and he turned to look across at Dusty, expecting to see an answering grin. There was none, only a cold hard and grim stare and a harsh:

"Keep your fool head down, this's no kid's game!"

Rusty moved fast, darting across the open space and flattening down by the other cowhand's side.

"You do what Dusty says," he warned.

"You in there!" Dusty barked out. "You behind the rocks. Throw out your guns and come on out with your hands raised."

"Go to hell!"

Pilbourne screamed the words back and fired a fast shot in the direction of where Dusty and Mark knelt. He jerked the rifle back and forced bullets into the breech, waiting and wondering what the cowhands meant to do.

"This's your last chance!" called Dusty.

The cowhand looked towards Rusty, surprised and said:

"I once saw a company of Texas Rangers taking a bad wanted man. The ranger captain sounded just like Dusty."

There was a grim smile on Rusty's face. "I was a deputy under him in Quiet Town just after the war. I tell you, Frank, no ranger captain could see the day when he can teach Dusty anything about handling something like this."

Behind their rock Dusty and Mark studied the situation. They thought as lawmen still, hard, tough and efficient lawmen. In the make-up of such men there was no taking foolish risks. They would face a man, even one in a position like this, alone, and chance being killed if they had to. Yet they would also take no chances and use the resources of all four men to take the killer now if the affair could be played that way.

"Reckon I could bounce a couple in on him, Dusty?" Mark asked.

"Make a try if you like," Dusty replied.

Mark aimed carefully, while Dusty and Rusty raised their own rifles ready to fire and hold Pilbourne down if he tried to retaliate. Mark fired, trying to send his bullet bouncing from the rock face and down on to the hidden man. The bullet flattened and left a leaden blotch on the wall. It did no damage. Nor did the next Mark threw and the big blond knew there was no chance of sending a ricochet in and dislodging the man.

"No go," said Dusty.

Behind the rock Pilbourne eased himself into a position where he hoped he would be able to shoot at the four men. His eyes went to the sky, it was gone noon and he could hold out until dark. Then there might be a chance to escape. He was alone and would take his chances in the dark against men who would hesitate to shoot for fear of hitting their friends.

The herd was moving along the draw now, the bedwagon already there and with Johnny loaded into it. Short handed as they were, the trail crew could not leave the cattle to see if they could help Dusty and the others. Pilbourne twisted around and got himself into a position where he could see and shoot down at the hands.

"Pull back or I'll cut down the riders!" he yelled.

Now there was a real urgent need to dislodge, either capture or kill the man or have their friends run the gauntlet of bullets from the rifle of a man who had proved he could call down his shots with some skill.

"Dusty!" Mark said suddenly. "Mind that time we were hunting cougar with your Cousin Betty? Just before we made that drive to Mulrooney?"

Dusty looked at his big friend and was about to growl out an angry demand as to the reason for the question. Then he recalled which hunt Mark meant, although it was far from the only hunt they'd had with Betty Hardin.

"Sure, I remember," he answered. "The dogs treed that ole cat and we couldn't see it. Then Betty saw the tip of its tail hanging down from the branches and she lined at———"

The words came to a halt as Dusty saw what Mark was getting at. From the edge of the rocks something black showed. It took Dusty just a bare split second to realise what that something was. The man behind the rock had moved, settled down to a safe shooting position where he could fire down on the trail below and in doing so was exposing the toe of one boot.

"You or me?" Dusty asked, without looking at Mark.

"My rifle likely hold closer," Mark replied. "But you're the better shot."

Dusty settled down and lined his carbine. It was a real tribute coming from Mark, who was a better than fair shot with the rifle. Mark knew that there was only one man living who might possibly equal the Kid in the skilled aiming of a long gun, and that man was Dusty Fog. The toe of the boot offered small enough target in all account and Mark knew there would be only the one shot at it.

"This's your last chance!" Dusty barked, even then not willing to kill the man if there was a chance of forcing him to surrender. "Come out or die."

Pilbourne had heard that kind of tone. It was a tough lawman speaking to a dangerous killer and meant every word said. He could come out and risk a trial, or he could force his play to the bitter end.

"I'll drop the point man!" he roared. "You make——"

The carbine lined, there was no time to ask again. Dusty knew without needing to look that Mark's rifle was lifted and ready to take up the second card of the deal. It was only left to Dusty to haul the ace from the hole and bring off the show-down, Dusty and that twenty inch barrelled Winchester carbine which the Kid always scoffed at as being grossly inaccurate at over ten feet.

The carbine spat and suddenly Pilbourne felt something strike his toes, sending agony through him, bringing a scream of pain from his lips as he reared up. The scream was cut off abruptly by the bark of Mark's rifle and the bullet it spewed out right straight into the up-jerking head. Pilbourne never knew what hit him; he spun, crashed into the wall behind him and went down.

Dusty, Mark and Rusty ran forward, but they came with their rifles held ready for instant use. They came from both sides, moving in fast towards where the killer was sprawled, arms thrown out and rifle laying well clear of him. If he had been holding the rifle they would have shot again, for that was how they were trained, never to trust a man who held a gun.

The cowhand watched the three men and wondered how he could have ridden with them for the past days without knowing all their traits. Rusty was acting like Dusty and Mark, acting like a well-trained lawman in this moment. The cowhand did not know of the hard lessons Dusty forced home on Rusty while they wore law badges in Quiet Town. Rusty had never forgotten those hard, firm rules Dusty laid down for dealing with a dangerous killer.

"He's cashed," Dusty said. "Cut down to the trail and ask Stone to hold the herd clear of the draw and get a couple of the boys back here."

Rusty went fast and Mark turned up the slope to collect the horses. Dusty looked down at the dead man's boot; the bullet had torn the sole badly and the toes were a bloody mess. The stitching of the upper was split and Dusty saw something white. He bent forward and extracted a sheet of paper the man had kept concealed in a hideout of a kind Dusty knew. Unfolding the paper, Dusty looked down the writing and read King Rambeau's death warrant signed by the saloon-keeper himself.

Stone Hart came up the slope as the herd came clear of the draw. He saw Dusty and Mark standing side by side, their faces grim and cold.

"Rambeau's men?" he asked.

"Sure, read this," Dusty replied.

Stone read the message and nodded grimly at the end. "How'll you handle it?"

"Ride on to Tombstone now," Dusty answered. "You're in the clear and likely be in tomorrow around noon. Mark and I'll deliver this, us and Lon."

"Lon's already gone," Stone drawled. "He doesn't know anything about this. Sent word with Rin he's gone to buy him a new Model '66."

"We'll likely find him," Dusty said gently, but there was no gentleness in his eyes. "Haul the bodies someplace and leave them for John Behan to look over—happens he wants to. They're renegades and there might be posters on them."

Stone watched Dusty and Mark mount their big horses. "I could spare Rusty and Doc," he said. "Rambeau's friendly with the Earp boys."

"I wouldn't spit in Wyatt's face if it was on fire," Dusty drawled as he turned the big paint stallion. "But I wouldn't see him backing a play like Rambeau just made."

"Not me," agreed Mark, reining his bloodbay around. "Not with certain proof like we've got against Rambeau. No sir, Stone, it wouldn't be Earp's play at all."

CHAPTER THIRTEEN

King Rambeau's Mistakes

Cindy Alban sat in the buggy, her arm around Miles Hamish's waist as he handled the reins. They'd been on a picnic and had completely forgotten how the time was flying. So now they headed slowly towards the distant lights of Tombstone not talking, each thinking. There was no show for them that night, for they were taking their last chance to relax before the opening of the Fair in two days' time.

The girl had a black Stetson hat on her head and wore a light dress under her coat. The night was not too cold and yet there was a bite in the air which made Hamish pleased that he'd brought his cloak with him. He swung it around his and the girl's shoulders, the white silk lining showing briefly in the night.

"Paula will be worrying," Cindy finally remarked. "I hope she doesn't send that young Earp boy out to look for us. This is the first time we've managed to throw him off and have a few moments alone."

"It's more than a few moments we've had," Hamish replied.

"We went out at noon and it's dark now. Young Earp has got it bad where you're concerned."

"I manage to hold him off," laughed Cindy.

Warren Earp, youngest of the brothers, had been one of Cindy's most constant attendants over the last few days. The girl liked him, found his boastings of travels to far-off cities like Sacramento or Saint Louis amusing. However, she did not care to have him around all the time as he tried to be. So it had been with something like relief that she slipped out of town and away from him for the picnic. He would undoubtedly be waiting at the boarding house, but she was sure he would now see he had no chance at all.

"I don't like having you out here after dark, Cindy."

"There's no danger this close to town," she answered.

"Howdy, Miss Cindy."

Hamish gave a startled exclamation and twisted around with his hand fanning towards his coat, where he had a shoulder holstered Merwin & Hulbert pocket revolver. The big white stallion had made no sound as it came up behind them and the first warning they'd been given was when the Ysabel Kid spoke. He'd seen them from a distance just before dark and only just caught up with them.

"Lon!" Cindy gasped.

Hamish brought his hand from under his coat and a smile came to his face, for he now knew that the Ysabel Kid was no rival. "I nearly shot you," he said.

"Folks're always doing that," came the Kid's drawling reply. "Must be something about me that makes 'em."

"My grandfather was a United States Customs Officer," Hamish answered, remembering stories he'd heard about the Kid's past. "That must be why——"

"Shucks, fancy admitting that afore a lady," chided the Kid. "Don't you hold it against him, Miss Cindy, he couldn't help it."

"I suppose not," Cindy replied. "And I could hardly hold it against Miles. You see, *my* father was head of the Border Patrol in Texas for a time after the War."

The Kid started to rein back his horse. "I knowed there was something about you pair that I didn't like."

The girl laughed and the Kid rode alongside the buggy again. The days when he rode as a border smuggler were long past, but his friends often teased him about them and he was never ashamed of the wild nights when he and his father ran contraband over the border.

For her part, Cindy was delighted that Miles Hamish was acting as he did. He was less stuffy and superior now and acting friendly with the Kid. It was at that moment the girl remembered what had happened to take the Kid from town.

"Where's the herd, Loncey?"

"Back there a piece. I came on ahead so I could hear you sigh."

The girl laughed and looked towards him, seeing that the big white stallion had covered a considerable amount of miles.

"Did you have any trouble bringing the herd this far?"

"Nope, not what I'd call real trouble."

For the rest of the ride Cindy tried to get the Kid to tell her some of the exciting things she was sure had happened. For all that, the Kid's version would have her believe the herd left Vance Brownlow's place and came through without anything worth talking about happening.

They reached the outskirts of Tombstone and made their way through the quiet backstreets to the boarding house. At Cindy's suggestion, the Kid left his leg-weary white stallion in an empty stall of the boarding house stables. Then with the white and the buggy team cared for the three walked towards the house.

The owner of the boarding house came to answer Hamish's knock. She looked out and her smile broadened as she looked at the girl, then faded a trifle at the sight of the unshaven, trail dusty young Texas cowhand who was with her.

"That's my friend, Loncey Dalton Ysabel," the girl remarked. "Can he wash up and tidy up in Miles' room, please?"

Cindy was the woman's favourite and could do no wrong. So the permission was willingly given and the Kid went with Hamish up the stairs. The woman stood looking at Cindy with a smile playing on her lips. The girl looked radiantly happy, her cheeks showing a touch of colour which was not entirely due to the Arizona sun.

"This Arizona climate seems to agree with you," she replied. "Miles is from New England, Warren Earp's from Iowa and the Kid's from Texas."

The Kid managed to get most of the dust from his clothes before he came down and found Cindy in the living room entertaining young Warren Earp. The youngest of the Earp brothers was a good-looking young man who wore cowhand dress and had a low-tied Colt holstered at his side. He was just removing the gunbelt when the Kid entered the room and frowned.

"Warren," Cindy said, leading him forward. "This is my friend, the Ysabel Kid."

Young Earp nodded a greeting and gave the Kid a broad grin. Doc Holliday was something of a hero to Warren Earp and from the deadly ex-dentist Warren had heard much about the Kid.

"Howdy, Kid," he greeted, then remembered the news which all Tombstone was awaiting. "Say, they were offering five to one that you didn't get that herd through Apache country."

"They were wrong," drawled the Kid. "She's got through and'll be here in a couple of days."

"Yowee, the men and old Doc's won us some money to bet on Brother Wyatt in the shooting matches."

Cindy felt relieved. She knew there was little love lost between the Earps and the cowhands and did not want trouble in the boarding house. Now it appeared the two young men were going to be friendly.

There was a knock on the outside door and the girl excused herself. She left the room, went along the passage and opened the door. A ragged Mexican boy stood outside, a piece of paper in his hand.

"For Señora Alban," he said.

The girl took the note, told the boy to come in while she found a coin to pay him. Then after seeing the boy depart she closed the door and opened out the paper. Her eyes went to the writing, read the first line and a hot flush came to her cheeks. The contents of the letter were vile, insulting in the worst degree that could be sprawned and poured out by King Rambeau's mind.

That was the moment when the saloon-keeper's plan started

to go wrong. His first mistake was in his judgement of Cindy Alban's character. The girl might allow herself to be saved from the villain when on the stage, but off it she was completely self-reliant. She was burning with a mixture of shame and anger at the message and determined to go along to Rambeau's saloon and shame him before the customers. She knew the ingrown chivalry of the Western men and knew that Rambeau's letter would be enough to see him run from Tombstone.

That was Rambeau's first mistake. He'd expected the girl to run to Miles Hamish with the letter. The two men outside the house were waiting for the young actor to come out, their orders to beat and mark him for life.

Cindy pulled her Stetson on, then she took Hamish's cloak from the hall stand and flipped it across her shoulders. Once the sun went down there often came a bit of cold in the air and she wanted the cloak, although her anger was warming her. She opened the door, the light in the hall behind her as she went out, the white silk lining of the cloak swinging out into view of the two men who stood by the gate. Miles Hamish was coming down the stairs from his room as the girl went out. He saw her closing the door and opened his mouth to call out.

In the darkness the two gunmen waited by the garden gate and there Rambeau's second mistake began. Neither of the men intended to risk a fist fight with the young actor, for they'd seen him bounce a drunken cowhand clear through the doors of the Bon Ton Theatre and were not meaning to tangle with him. The end product would be the same. The rest of the show were attending some function in town and the two gunmen expected the girl to come running out when she heard the sounds of Hamish being worked over. Their orders were to grab Cindy and take her to a cabin on the edge of Tombstone, where Rambeau would collect her.

One of the gunmen lifted his gun as he saw the shape come through the door. He knew that cloak and the Stetson hid any sign of Cindy's hair from his view. He brought up the Colt and fired, saw the shape at the door stagger and went through the gate.

Then hell broke loose.

Hamish heard the shot, saw the door panel split as a bullet

came through and heard a shrill scream of pain. Then he was hurling down the stairs and towards the door, and even as he tore it open he heard a crash of glass from the next room.

The Ysabel Kid was pacing the room. He was never really at home in such a place as this boarding house. He passed the window and through a slit in the curtains saw two shapes by the garden gate. He gave it no thought and crossed to the door of the room, glanced at Cindy as she was putting the cloak on. Warren Earp was seated, relaxed and at home, watching the cat-like way the Kid prowled the room. He opened his mouth to say something as the Kid went to the window again. Then he saw the Kid tense, heard the shot and started to come to his feet.

The Kid brought both hands in front of his face and went straight through the window, carrying sash and glass with him in passing. He hit the ground outside, making havoc among the owner's flower bed. His old Dragoon Colt was gripped in his hand as he saw one of the two men running forward and heard the startled curse as the man saw it was Cindy and not Hamish he'd shot.

Even as the Kid started to bring up his Dragoon he saw the house door burst open and Miles Hamish hurl out. Full on to the gunman, clearing the girl's weakly moving body, hurled the young actor. The revolver crashed once wildly, sending the bullet into the ground, then the gunman was smashed down with a savage fighting fury on him, battering him with hard fists.

The second gunman had seen the Kid come through the window and his Colt was listed, but against the darkness of the house the black clothing worked as a cloak of invisibility and nothing of the Kid showed as he tensed, ready to move in and take the gunman.

The gunman could see nothing but a whirling tangle as Miles Hamish and his companion fought. He could not risk a shot at them. Then he saw a second shape at the window and his Colt crashed. Young Warren Earp had leapt to the window, making a basic mistake; his gun was in his hand ready, but the bullet which came from the night taught him a lesson. He spun around, his shirt torn wide open and a bloody gash appearing on the flesh of his shoulder. With a yell of pain the young man spun around, back against the wall and out of sight.

The Kid was halfway across the garden before the gunman saw him. The man began his turn, but flame blossomed from the barrel of the old Dragoon even before any action could be taken. The gunman let out a scream of pain as the bullet caught him high in the shoulder, smashing flesh and bone as only a round, soft lead ball powered by a full forty grain charge of prime Du Pont powder could. The gunman was thrown backwards, hit the ground and lay screaming in agony, his arm almost torn from his body.

By now the owner of the house and other people from along the street were coming, carrying lamps and lighting up a scene they would never forget. Cindy was holding her shoulder, crouched against the door, with her face white as she stared at Miles Hamish, who knelt beside the man who shot her and smashed his head brutally on to the hard soil of the path.

The Kid came forward, his Dragoon in his hands, the hammer drawn back under his thumb. "Get off him, friend," said his voice, the growling snarl of a Comanche Dog Soldier taking his lodge oath.

Miles Hamish looked up with unseeing eyes. His left hand knotted into the man's hair, his right came across to smash knuckled into the bloody face. The head crashed on to the path with a satisfactory thud and Hamish gripped the head once more.

The Kid had no intention of stopping Hamish killing the man, that was for sure. To him it was nothing that did not require doing and the young actor had the right to do it. The other people were gathering around fast, some looking down at the badly wounded gunman in the street, others crowding into the garden, where the boarding house owner was already bending over Cindy.

Weakly the girl forced herself up and gasped, "Miles! Miles, stop it!"

Possibly there was not another thing in the world which could have stopped the young actor's blind and savage rage. He heard the voice and released the man's head, allowing it to drop back to the path. Then, rising, he turned and went to Cindy, dropping on his knees beside her.

The girl was hit high in the shoulder; it was a painful and

nasty wound, but she would live. Her eyes were open, full of pain and not a touch of pride in the way Miles went to save her. The kneeling woman, by Cindy's side, looked at the neighbours who were running up the path and took command of the situation.

"Miles, carry Cindy inside and watch her shoulder," she snapped. "Mrs. O'Neil, would you be so kind as to go for the doctor?"

The Ysabel Kid stood in the garden for a moment, then something white caught his eye. He stepped forward and picked up the note which brought Cindy through the door. The people who were close at hand saw him open it and glance at the writing in the light of the lamp. Then they saw the change which came over his face. No longer was it the innocent, handsome, yet somewhat babyish face of the Ysabel Kid. Now it was the war-mask of a Comanche looking for an enemy.

Warren Earp was by the door, holding his bloody flesh wound. He saw the Kid crumple the paper and asked, "Who were they, Kid?"

"Rambeau's men," the Kid answered and went to where men were gathered around his victim in the street. There was no chance of questioning the other man, he was unconscious and would stay that way for some time. The man the Kid shot was conscious, though only just, and he was in agony. The Kid shoved by the watching men and bent down. He knotted his fist into the man's shirt and hauled him into a sitting position, bringing a scream from him. "Who sent you?"

The gunman screamed again and gasped out, "Rambeau!"

For a moment the Kid stood holding the wounded, screaming gunman with his left hand, right curled around the butt of the old Dragoon Colt. There were big men in the crowd, tough men, but not one of them would have dared to interfere. Go up against a she-bear with new-born cubs, go into a cave where a scared cougar was in hiding; but go against the Ysabel Kid at this moment and the other two would seem like nothing.

Dropping the man's shirt and allowing him to fall back to the ground, the Kid turned. The man was a cheap gunman, just a trigger to be pulled. His arm would never be of use to him again. He had been punished enough. It was the man behind the trigger who must pay.

Turning on his heel, the Kid glanced towards the house and to where Warren Earp was pushing through the onlookers.

"They were doing it for Rambeau," said the Kid gently, yet there was no gentleness in his tone.

"Can I help you?" asked the youngest Earp.

"Get your shoulder seen to, Warren. I'll tend to Rambeau."

Before Warren Earp could open his mouth to either object or warn the Kid that Rambeau had several men at his place, it was too late. The Kid was walking along the once quiet, now disturbed street, making for the King Saloon, where he was going to kill a man or die in the trying.

The shooting brought Virgil Earp, but he came from the other direction and so missed the Kid. From his younger brother he learned of what happened and looked along the street to where the Kid was already out of sight. A man came from the house with word that Cindy had fainted but was in no serious danger. Virgil Earp stood looking at his brother's wound and a hard, grim look came to his face.

"I thought we'd taught you better," he said. "Coming in front of a window with a light behind you. Say—Wyatt, Morgan, Bat Masterson and Doc Holliday are at Rambeau's place."

"We'd best get down there, they might side Rambeau," Warren answered.

"I'll go," Virgil snapped. "You stay here, get that shoulder tended to, then move those two gunmen down to the jail."

Even as he turned, Virgil Earp knew he would be too late. One thing was sure, no matter which way this thing went, King Rambeau was done in Tombstone. It would do the Law and Order Party no good to be friendly with the man who caused the shooting of Cindy Alban, a favourite of the Bon Ton Theatre and darling of every man in the wild and sprawling town.

The King Saloon was booming open. Rambeau moved through the crowd, greeted his friends, or those who were in such a position as to make it worth while to appear friendly.

The batwing doors of the saloon opened and Rambeau felt a sudden cold and raw ache of fear biting into him. This was yet another mistake he'd made. He had not known the Ysabel Kid was in town. In that moment Rambeau knew that his plan had gone wrong, although the noise of the four-piece band, laughter, sounds of his place, had drowned down the shots.

"Rambeau!" the Kid's voice cut across the room. "It didn't work, you lousy, no-good yellow rat."

The first word came in a slight lull of the noise and with each succeeding word the silence grew. The roulette wheel clicked unheeded to a halt, the laughter and curses at the vingt-un table ended, the band trailed off to a discordant chord and died away.

Rambeau knew what had happened, knew that his plan was wrong, knew it from the slip of paper in the hand of the Ysabel Kid. He was near to the Earp brothers' table and threw them a look, but so far Wyatt was not taking cards, was sitting fast until he knew what was wrong and where public opinion lay before cutting in.

"What's eating you?" Rambeau asked, knowing his men were moving in ready to help him.

"Your boys shot Miss Alban, reckon it might have been a mistake, but they shot her."

The words carried to every man in the crowd and the silence was more deeply ominous than ever before. Rambeau could feel the soft, cold hand of death on him and knew he must kill the Kid before too much could be said. There was enough on that sheet of paper to hang him and he knew it. His eyes went across the room to where his last two gunmen were moving through the crowd, making to where they could flank and side him.

The gunmen moved forward, then a foot came up, across the gap between the two tables they were passing. They halted, eyes going to the leg which was so clearly blocking their passage. Then they looked along it, up by the gambler's coat from under which showed the butt of a shot-pistol, up to the sallow face of Doc Holliday. The thin killer's lips drew back in a grim and he shook his head gently.

"That's private, boys. Let's keep it that way."

Rambeau saw what had happened to his gunmen, saw it and knew they were out of the game unless they fixed to tie in with Doc Holliday. He knew, however, the rest of the saloon workers would back him, thinking they were tying in on a matter for the Syndicate. The odds were good, the crowd moving back and allowing his own men to come forward and make a half-circle behind him. They were not professional gunmen, all worked in some capacity in the saloon, but they could all use their guns and no one man could stand against them.

Wyatt Earp shoved back his chair and came to his feet; with two brothers, the tall, derby hatted, Eastern dressed Bat Masterson and Rambeau's men backing him he ought to be able to stop the Ysabel Kid from causing trouble. It would be something of a feather in his cap if he could.

"You'd best go out to Mrs. Satterlee's boarding house, Earp," the Kid spoke evenly. "Warren took a bullet in the shoulder in the shooting."

One of the few good points any Texan was willing to concede about the Earp brothers was their loyalty to the family. Cut one Earp and all the brothers bled. Morgan Earp was now on his feet by his brother's side.

"What're you meaning, Kid?" he asked.

"Rambeau here sent two men to wait outside where Cindy Alban is living. He sent her this note, thought either Miles Hamish or me would get shown it and come out to be killed. Only Cindy didn't show it us. She put Miles' cloak on and started to come down here, reckon she aimed to face this stinking rat down and show him for what he is—only she didn't make it. One of them shot her as she came through the door."

There was a rumble of anger at the Kid's words. His left hand lifted and he threw the paper towards the Earps. Morgan caught it but did not open it, he was more concerned about his brother.

"What about Warren?"

"Like I said, he caught a bullet from one of Rambeau's men."

"Is that true, Rambeau?" Morgan growled.

"I don't know what the hell he's talking about."

Rambeau could feel the touch of the hold-out and the stubby Remington Double Derringer. It was his chance to finish the Kid before he could say any more. His hand twitched and he was about to press the spring to send the grip of the little gun into his waiting palm. The saloon workers would back him even now if he moved fast.

The batwing doors of the saloon opened and two men stepped

in. Two Texan men, one tall, one short, but both wearing two guns and both alike in their cold and deadly menace as they flanked the Ysabel Kid.

"We got your hired men, Rambeau," said Dusty Fog. "You played the wrong card when you wrote out that agreement."

"He's mine, Dusty," warned the Kid.

It was at that moment Rambeau found he stood alone. The saloon workers were not gunmen, but they knew who these two men were. This was the small Texan who had beaten Iowa Parsons to the shot and the big Texan who, by all accounts, had brought his gun clear of leather before Rambeau's best gun, top hired killer of the Syndicate, cleared leather.

Rambeau felt the sweat run down his face. The Earp brothers were walking out of the saloon, going to see how badly Warren was hurt. Bat Masterson and Doc Holliday were still here, but both showed they'd no intention of siding with him. It now all stood or fell on him. He was done and there was nothing but a rope before him unless he could kill the Ysabel Kid.

"Three to one?" he asked, fighting wildly for a chance.

Dusty Fog turned and walked to one side, halting with his hands resting on the top of the nearby vingt-un table. Mark Counter swung away, also presenting his back as he went and sat with Bat Masterson, not looking around and in no position to bring rapid aid to his friend. At the same moment the saloon workers faded back. Now they knew this was no Syndicate matter and Rambeau stood alone in it.

"One to one, start when you like," drawled the Ysabel Kid.

Rambeau pressed the spring catch of the hold-out, felt the Derringer flick down and into his hand. He started to bring the weapon up in a fast move even as the Kid twisted his hand palm out to lift clear the old Dragoon. Then Rambeau hesitated, the short barrelled hide-out gun lining. Was he aiming at the Kid, could he be sure of a hit? The thoughts raced through his mind in that flickering second between the Kid gripping the old Dragoon and bringing it out to line. Only a brief time did the man hesitate—but it was long enough.

Never, by the wildest stretch of imagination could the Ysabel Kid claim he was fast with a gun. It took him all of a second, starting from empty hand and ending with lead flying, for him to make his draw and a second was a whole lot too long at a time like this.

The old Dragoon came up even as Rambeau hesitated, trying to decide if the Derringer was lined. Flame lashed from the old Colt in the Kid's hand, there was no hesitation about the heavy .44 ball and Rambeau went backwards, arms flailing, into the table behind it, fell onto it, rolled off and to the floor.

There was not a sound through the saloon as all eyes went to King Rambeau, who had just made his final mistake.

The batwing doors opened and Virgil Earp stepped in. He came quietly and without hurry, but he came with his hands held well clear of his belt. A man did not take chances when dealing with a situation such as had been enacted in the King Saloon. The Ysabel Kid was too fast to take any chances with when he'd just dropped a man and might suspect anyone who came behind him.

The Kid turned, holstering his Colt as a sign of his good faith and Virgil Earp felt relieved. The Texas memory of Kansas towns did not tend to give any son of the Lone Star State trust in any man who bore the name of Earp. Virgil stepped forward with a nod towards Rambeau's body and the crowd saw there would be nothing more happen.

"You got him, Kid," he said. "Miss Alban's all right. She'll live, be off the stage for a time, but she'll live."

"You'd best take a look at this," replied the Kid and handed over the note Rambeau sent to Cindy.

Dusty and Mark were by their friend now and from the pocket of his shirt Dusty took a second sheet of paper.

"You'd best take this while you're at it."

Earp read the two notes and the crowd moved forward trying to hear everything that was said. Slowly Virgil Earp looked up after he read the two notes. One he could understand, the one which brought the end to Rambeau's life at the hands of the Ysabel Kid. The other puzzled him and he asked about it.

"I took it from one of the gang of renegades who hit at the herd some ways back, at that draw," Dusty explained. "Reckon you'll find it's in Rambeau's hand if you take a look in his office."

The story of the drive came out, bringing whispered remarks

of admiration from the crowd. The fight at the draw was glossed over, but there was an angry rumble at the Kid's old yellow rifle. Every man in the saloon knew that the Kid was one of the top favourites in the shooting, or had been. His chances of coming anywhere with his old, tired and trusted rifle bust were small.

The problem was worrying the Kid and Mark Counter moved forward from the crowd. They stood looking at each other for a moment, not noticing Doc Holliday stood close behind them, listening to every word.

"You've used my Model '73," Mark said quietly.

The Kid nodded in agreement. He'd used Mark's rifle on more than one occasion, but that did not give him the knowledge he would need of its ways to enable him to win the Rifle Match.

"Happen I could take it out of town for a couple of days, with plenty of bullets, I might learn how it fires in time."

"That'd be easy arranged."

"It'd cost more money than I've got to spare."

Mark dipped his hand into his pocket and grinned wryly. "I near on spent out myself."

Holliday turned back to look around the room. His eyes fell on the roulette table, where the dealer was idly spinning the wheel ready to start business once more when the crowd returned. Crossing the room, Holliday removed his wallet and tossed a pile of notes on the table, landing them casually on the seven. The dealer looked up and the cold eyes of the killer brought an uncomfortable and uneasy chill to him.

"Your boss caused the Kid's rifle to be bust," said Holliday. "Reckon it's only right he helps make up for it. I'm betting one hundred and fifty dollars to help him."

The dealer grinned. He'd got ten dollars riding on the Ysabel Kid's rifle skill and hoped Doc Holliday called his guess right. With a practised flick of the wrist he started the wheel spinning with one hand, the other going to the small marble ball. Then Holliday spoke, his voice mild, gentle and yet cold and freezing as the bite of a Texas blue norther storm.

"We don't need to bother with that—now do we?"

Slowly the dealer's eyes went to Holliday's face, then to the thin hand as it hovered the butt of the shot pistol. He let the ball rest on top of the wheel spindle and his tongue tip flickered across his lips.

"No sur, Doc, I don't reckon we do. Seven's the winner."

The Ysabel Kid and Mark Counter were still wondering how they could get around the money problem and if Frank Leslie or Texas John Slaughter could help them lay in a supply of bullets.

"Kid," the word brought them both around to face Doc Holliday. "Here, take this. See that fat jasper playing vingt-un? Go tell him I said for him to sell you anything you want."

The Kid accepted the money, asking no questions. He knew Doc Holliday slightly and wondered what made the killer give him a pile of notes. Then he glanced to the vingt-un table and the fat, prosperous looking townsman who was playing. The crowd were rapidly getting back to the interrupted pleasures now.

"Reckon he'll do it, Doc?" asked the Kid.

Doc Holliday grinned. "I reckon he will. Just tell him I saw him in Bignose Kate's last week, while his wife was on vacation."

So it was that at dawn the following morning the Ysabel Kid rode out of Tombstone with Mark Counter's Model 1873 Winchester, the packhorse, his white stallion and over a hundred and fifty dollars' worth of cartridges. He had the first five days of the fair and all the Sunday to learn enough about the centerfire rifle to let him enter the Rifle Match and win that magnificent "One in a Thousand" Winchester.

CHAPTER FOURTEEN

The Cochise County Fair

The Cochise County Fair had been a roaring success so far. It came up to all its organisers had hoped for. From the East, brought from the railheads in the best and most comfortable coaches Wells Fargo could supply, came the rich dudes, eager to see the wild, wide open town of Tombstone at play. They flocked in and with them came much money to be spent over bars, in the hotels, at the gambling tables.

The dudes came, stared with amazement and delight as steel thewed miners sank steel drill bits into the rock and hard soil. They cheered to delight as Chow Willicka of the Wedge drove his lathered chuck wagon team to victory in a thrilling race. They watched, trying to imitate the wild cowhand yells as bucking horses were rode and riders piled into the dirt. They stared at the men who would provide the main attraction, the Pistol Shoot. Tall Tom Horn, in buckskins and looking like a bold Apache war chief. Bat Materson, in derby hat and eastern clothes, but with a brace of Colts in a fast man's rig. Wyatt Earp, looking for all the world like a prosperous trail-end town undertaker. Burt Alvord, who the dudes whispered behind their hands, had been a lawman who never brought in a living prisoner. The dude ladies sighed and fanned their faces vigorously when that blond giant, that rangeland dandy from Texas, Mark Counter, strolled by or attended some function to which the ladies were invited. There was a man, what a man. The mild faced dudes paled into nothing in comparison with such a man.

Walking the crowded streets with Mark Counter was a small man, a nobody in the eyes of the dudes, and few, if any, asked his name. Those who did were surprised when told he was *the* Captain Dusty Fog of Civil War and later fame. The dudes who were told this laughed, suspected that they were being jobbed, as was known to be the Western custom. Few, if any, of the dudes bet their money on that small, soft talking and insignificant Texan. For this Buckskin Frank Leslie and other odds giving gentlemen were grateful.

The day of the rifle shoot dawned clear and fine, there was little wind and conditions were ideal for shooting. The Ysabel Kid had returned that morning early, paid a visit to Cindy Alban who, with arm in a sling, was able to walk around. Then he went to the line in a shooting match which would long be talked about in the West.

It is possible that no man ever was at such great disadvantage as was the Kid when he went out to the line with Mark Counter's rifle under his arm and the remains of the ammunition he took from town with him. Where he'd been and what he'd done with the rest he never told anyone and there were few who would have dared to ask.

The match was arranged so that there was an emphasis on the fast handling and repeating quality of the Winchester and such rifles, and one rule was that the same rifle must be used all through. This rather put a block on Wyatt Earp's plan to use his Winchester for the ordinary shooting but to bring in a Sharps Old Reliable when accuracy over a long distance was called for.

Details of the match were reported on by the *Tombstone Epitaph* and repeated in papers throughout the length and breadth of the United States. The editor of the paper began in grand terms to describe the scene, meaning to carry on with how his friend Wyatt Earp cleared all before him. By the time the first three parts of the shoot were over it was clear that, good though Earp was, that black dressed boy from Texas was much better.

For all of that, the Ysabel Kid did not get everything his own way. The rifle in his hands was still strange to him and he had to concentrate all the time to remember the traits he'd learned on his lonely ride for the past days. Let him but relax for one moment and he slipped back to handling the rifle in the manner of his broken old yellow boy. It cost him points and kept the crowd in a state of tension. So much so that on the last shoot it was still possible for any of the others to take the Kid's precariously held lead from him.

The last test would be the one which would decide who owned that wonderful rifle and an engraver specially sent out by the Winchester company was seated poised and ready to carve the name of the winner on the silver plate. It was a test which would bring out the finest qualities of the men who now stood on the line. There were only eight men left and the crowd was tense as they waited.

At a distance of some twenty feet before each man lay a spread out handkerchief; beyond this were three foot high hurdles spaced some five feet apart. The idea was to fire bullets so close as to bounce the handkerchiefs into the air, over the hurdles, in the fewest shots and faster than the other contestants.

The Kid relaxed on the line, the tensions of competition not bothering him as he gave Cindy Alban a wave. The starter for the event raised his hand, his Colt pointing into the air.

"Are you ready, gentlemen?" he asked and received the nods in agreement. "Get set, then go!"

The word was echoed by the deep bark of his Colt and re-echoed by the flat barks of eight rifles. The eight handkerchiefs were bounced into the air, sailing up by the force of the close landing bullets. On his third shot Burt Alvord pulled off slightly and his bullet ripped through the handkerchief, at which he aimed. He was out, the handkerchief, torn by the shattering impact of the bullet, resisted all his efforts to bounce it again.

The Kid's eyes focused along the barrel of the rifle. The bouncing handkerchief was a gaudy hue which reminded him of his friend Red Blaze's bandanna. The various colours caught the eye and were easy to pick out, but they had the disadvantage of blurring and becoming indistinct, making the exact place to aim at hard to locate. For all of that, the Kid's third shot bounced the handkerchief over the first hurdle before any of the others made it. The Kid's sighting eye never made any mistake and slowly the mumble of the crowd grew. He was over the second hurdle and there were only three men left in it now. Wyatt Earp was throwing his shots fast, trying to catch up on the Kid's lead. His very haste caused him to miss a chance, his handkerchief hung over the second hurdle, caught on it, resisting three fast thrown bullets to tear it free.

The Kid's eleventh shot sent the handkerchief into the air; it spread out and came down. There was a gasp of dismay from the onlookers, for the handkerchief had caught by its very tip on the face side of the hurdle. Tom Horn, last man in the contest, saw this and fired again; the handkerchief before him sailed into the air and fell short of the hurdle, just too close for him to hope to bounce it over, but he lined his rifle. The Kid was also sighting and the crowd held his concerted breath. The two shots sounded almost as one and the crowd let out a yell which rang out and threw back echoes.

Tom Horn's handkerchief hung over the top of the hurdle. From the Kid's hurdle had burst a shower of splinters and the handkerchief tore free to float down on the other side. With a wry grin Tom Horn lowered his smoking Winchester and spread his hand in the Indian sign talk way of saying finished.

A band started to blare out a stirring tune. The civic dignitaries of Tombstone crowded forward eagerly. In a tent the Winchester engraver was poised ready to work. The judge of the match emptied the Kid's rifle magazine and counted the remaining bullets, then did the same for Tom Horn. The big buckskin man was grinning, knowing he had fired more shots than had the Kid.

Slowly the referee raised his right hand, the band gave a final roaring fanfare and silence that could almost be felt spread over the crowd.

"Ladies and gentlemen," announced the judge in a booming shout which carried over the vast crowd. "The winner of the Cochise County Fair's Rifle Shoot and winner of the One of a Thousand Winchester Model 1873 rifle I give you, Number Ten on your programme, Loncey Dalton Ysabel."

The crowd gave out their approval in traditional style, from the dudes came polite and well-bred applause, from the miners cheers of louder and more raucous style. It was from the cowhands that the most noise came. Those hardy sons of the saddle bellowed out their wild yells, fired their Colts into the air in their delight. The "yeeah!" battle yell of the Confederate Army rang out loud and clear, and for once the Ysabel Kid's face showed its true feelings.

It was only with a considerable effort that the Kid restrained his impatience to get hold of the magificent Winchester which was brought from the tent where the Winchester engraver had done his work fast and with skill.

Holding the rifle, the Mayor of Tombstone began a speech, praising the Kid's shooting skill and tossing in a few words of praise for his town, the Fair and for Cochise County in general. Then he held out the rifle and the Kid, trying to look normal and nonchalant, as if winning such a wonderful rifle was an every-day thing, took it. From the first moment of gripping it the rifle felt good in the Kid's hands. He slipped bullets into the breech and at a word from the Mayor stepped forward on to the firing line. A man ran down the line of hurdles and placed three beer bottles on the farthest, just where the handkerchief had hung. He moved to one side and the Mayor nodded.

Up came the "One of a Thousand" Winchester, the Kid's eyes lining along the barrel, his finger caressing the set trigger. The flat crack of the Winchester was followed by two more in quick succession, but with each shot one of the bottles was burst by the bullet.

"Yes, sir, Mr. Mayor," drawled the Kid. "That's a tolerable close shooting rifle."

The crowd were wild in their cheers of delight, yelling their approval, and the Kid walked to where his two friends waited for him. He handed Mark back the rifle he'd used for the match and grinned. Dusty was also grinning.

"Lon," he said. "I never saw you look like this since that day when Tom Alden gave you that yellow boy just after the War."

"I never thought to own a rifle like this," replied the Kid. "Let's get out on the range and see how close she shoots."

Dusty shook his head. "We're all invited to a dinner by

Vance Brownlow and his good lady. And I promised on my word as a Texan that you'd be there."

"Which same means you'll be there all right," Mark went on. "Likewise, I gave Miz Birdie my solemn oath you'd be along."

The Kid grinned and cursed the unguarded moment when he let Birdie Brownlow know his aversion to attending formal dinners. He also recollected that he had annoyed her and Chow both with his comments on their cooking, and this appeared to be a way of getting their revenge on him. The thought was confirmed soon after when the old cook came ambling up.

"Hear tell you coming to this fancy dinner tonight, Kid," he said, then leered at the Indian dark face. "I always telled you evil got paid back in the end."

Cackling hoarsely, Chow Willicka ambled on and the Kid made a mental note never to rile Chow again—unless he was sure there was a good avenue of escape left for him.

The dinner was far from being as formal as the Kid imagined, although there was a fair crowd along for it, the trail crew, Vance, his wife, all Madam Paula's troupe, several town dignitaries and a few dudes who had managed to get themselves invited.

After the meal the men stood around talking while preparing for the show Madam Paula promised them. Dusty leaned by the bar at the corner of the room. He was looked over by the Dudes and passed off as some minor member of the trail drive drew, although the same dudes were puzzled at the deference the others showed to this small and insignificant Texan.

Sheriff John Behan, one of the guests, joined Dusty, a broad grin on his face. Jerking his thumb towards the editor of the *Tombstone Epitaph,* he said, "Clem looks real down in the mouth. The Kid spoiled a good story for him."

"Likely, John, likely," answered Dusty. "Wyatt Earp's not here."

"Nor likely to be," Behan replied. "He got to boasting about winning just after you pulled out, so I made a bet with him. Things stand this way, if he loses both the shoots he doesn't stand for sheriff against me."

Dusty looked at the other man for a long moment, then grinned. "That was a mite tricky, John."

"Like my pappy always told me, Cap'n Dusty, if you can't lick 'em, trick 'em."

At that moment the show started and for the first time the Ysabel Kid managed to hear Cindy Alban sing. Later that same evening the Kid's pleasant untrained tenor voice was matched in duets with the girl, but she had eyes only for Miles Hamish and on the third finger of her left hand was a diamond ring.

The following morning found an air of expectation over the crowd as they moved out of Tombstone to the place where the shooting would be performed. There were only nine men left in now, the others had realised they stood no chance and so bowed out.

There was some talk among the crowd when the contestants lined up for the first shots. Wyatt Earp had his long barrelled Peacemaker holstered at his left side and all there knew a fast draw was impossible with such a weapon but it would give him a good chance of scoring well in the long range work.

The first tests rolled by, shooting with sights and by rough alignment at targets, then at a can thrown into the air. Earp scored well, so did all the other men, but when the scores were added it was found that the small man who was marked down at number nine was the highest scorer of them all and next to him that blond giant called Mark Counter.

"That long range work will show a difference," Vance Brownlow remarked to Stone Hart as they stood in the forefront of the crowd, watching a man who was setting up an empty whisky bottle in the center of a patch of cleared earth some hundred yards from the firing point.

"Likely," drawled Stone. "Likely. I'd still bet on Dusty for it."

By the time Earp took his stand no man had managed to hit the bottle in less than five shots. There was a grin on Earp's face as he lined the long barrelled Colt and fired, watching the dust puff up where the bullet slapped into the earth near the bottle. There was a rumble of approval from the watching crowd, for no other man had come so close to the bottle with his first shot. Earp stood sideways, holding the Colt shoulder high as he sighted. His second shot dusted the bottle but did not break it. On the third shot there was a crash and a flying hail of splintered glass, and cheers rang out from Earp's supporters. Here was one part of the ranch they were sure he would win.

Mark Counter took his place with the seven and a half inch barrelled Cavalry Peacemaker in his right hand. His first shot was just as close in as Earp's, but it took Mark four shots to hit the bottle. The third shot had been close, it should have been a hit by all fair means, but the four and a half inch difference in the gun barrels gave Earp a big advantage. Mark grinned and walked back to where Dusty stood. The big Texan was satisfied, although now Earp stood slightly over him in the scoring. There was the test for fast gun handling next and Earp's long barrelled gun would put him at a disadvantage.

There was a mutter from the crowd as they saw the type of Colt Dusty was using. It had taken Bat Masterson six shots to range in the four and three-quarter inch barrel of a Civilian Model Peacemaker and none of the crowd thought to see the small Texan do any better.

Dusty sighted carefully, watching how the breeze stirred the grass, then made his calculations and cocked back the hammer. Another pause to make sure of the aim, then Dusty fired. There was a roar from the crowd as dust erupted within a scant inch of the bottle. For a moment every one of the crowd thought a hit was scored and a yell rolled high then died away.

Unruffled by the noise, Dusty set his sights again, waiting for a moment when the breeze was at its steadiest. There was not a sound from the whole crowd as the people waited for the crack of the Peacemaker. Then Dusty fired! The bottle burst, shattering under the impact of the .45 bullet.

It took the crowd a long five seconds to realise what had happened. Then, as Wyatt Earp threw down his cigar in disgust, the cheers rolled out.

Earp's temper did not improve on the test for fast gunhandling. For this the contestant walked down a valley and targets, mansized and shaped, were pulled up from behind cover with the aid of ropes. He shot well, but knew that he might have scored even better. This was the event for which the long barrelled Peacemaker was the prize, and he hoped to take it. However, Mark Counter scored higher, getting the highest points so far. Dusty followed and went the line of the valley, shooting fast and equalling Mark's score.

"Toss you for it," Mark drawled as they walked towards the judges.

"Spin a coin and make a call," Dusty answered.

Mark laughed, flipped a coin into the air and made a correct call, so he took the cased presentation Peacemaker.

It was now, as the men went to the line for the last event, that the interest of the crowd really worked up. The other shooting had been good, very good, but it was something they could have seen any time. Right now was the big moment, the star attraction which the organisers of the Fair planned. This was the test to see who was the fastest man with a gun.

The Colt company had been hard put to think of a way to test the speed of the draw and after much thought came up with an idea. To one side of where the shooting had taken place the special targets were set up. They were mansized and cut in the shape of a man drawing a gun. The posts on which these targets were fixed rested on, but were not fastened to, a bar. Beyond this and placed so that the target support would hit it when moved by the force of a bullet, was a second bar with spring-loaded grips attached so as to catch and hold the target supports. The target line was made so that the first shot to hit a target moved it and the support back to hit the second bar. This in turn loosened the spring loaded grips on to the other targets and prevented them from falling over backwards.

In tests conducted both at Hartford and on the ground at Tombstone the system showed it worked even when there were only split seconds between the impacts. It was possible to tell which bullet hit first, for that was the only target which could fall over.

The nine men took their places on the line. Each one was set, making sure his holstered Colts lay just right. They were probably the fastest men alive, those who toed that line, each one having proved his right to be there, with a smoking Colt in the heat of a gunbattle. This would settle one argument, who was the fastest of them all.

"Gentlemen!" boomed the judge of the match, holding a Colt in his right hand, "I'll count to three, then fire a shot. On that shot you make your move."

The line of men stood ready, hands poised to grip the butts of their guns. The count was given, then the Colt crashed. As if springs were released, hands snapped down. Dusty's hands crossed, the curve of the Peacemaker butts fitting into his palms as they so often had before. There was no conscious effort about the move, no straining to gain extra speed. The thumbs curved over the hammers, drawing them back to firing position even as the Colts cleared leather. Dusty's eyes were on the target before him, twenty feet away, the guns came up and lined to fire while still waist high. The thunder of his Colts sounded and was lost in the crash of the other eight men's weapons, which came as a ragged crash. Dusty saw his target rock back, saw the others jerk, then his target tipped over and crashed to the ground.

The crowd were silent for a moment, then wild were the whoops and yells from those watching Texans, the other cowhands joining in. Every cowhand here was wild with delight, for one of their kind, one of the leading names of their trade, had just proved he was the fastest gun of them all.

Dusty holstered his Colts as the yells and cheers of the crowd died away to allow the judge to announce the winner. He was smiling, this small Texan, knowing that the test proved little or nothing. It was one thing to send a bullet into a target but another again to throw lead at a man who might be faster and was capable of throwing bullets back. Dusty Fog knew that the crowd would not think of that, they had seen Wyatt Earp, Bat Masterson and the other fast men beaten by the Rio Hondo gun wizard. Arizona was safe from the Kansas lawmen.